Desert Heart

The Wolves of Twin Moon Ranch
Book 4

by Anna Lowe

Twin Moon Press

Editing by Lisa A. Hollett

Covert art by Fiona Jayde

Contents

Other books in this series

The Wolves of Twin Moon Ranch

Desert Hunt (the Prequel)

Desert Moon (Book 1)

Desert Blood (Book 2)

Desert Fate (Book 3)

Desert Heart (Book 4)

Desert Rose (Book 5)

Desert Roots (Book 6)

Desert Yule (a short story)

Desert Wolf: Complete Collection (Four short stories)

Sasquatch Surprise (a Twin Moon spin-off story)

visit www.annalowebooks.com

Free Books

Get your free e-books now!

Sign up for my newsletter at *annalowebooks.com* to get three free books!

- *Desert Wolf*: Friend or Foe (Book 1.1 in the Twin Moon Ranch series)

- *Off the Charts* (the prequel to the Serendipity Adventure series)

- *Perfection* (the prequel to the Blue Moon Saloon series)

Chapter One

Tina pulled in a long, steadying breath, wishing she could tell her brother to do the same. He drove the pickup down the rutted dirt road, muttering and glaring at every bush. Another five minutes of that and it wouldn't surprise her if one of them burst into flames. His left hand was clenched white on the wheel; his right scratched at his ear.

"Damn ranch."

He didn't mean Twin Moon Ranch—their home, their legacy. A place their father had toiled over for more than a century. Under the leadership of her brothers, Twin Moon pack was prospering. Their finances were solid, the future promising.

No, Ty wasn't cursing over things at home. He was cursing the neighboring property. Seymour Ranch.

So many memories there. So much heartache.

Tina wound a length of her hair around her finger and tried sending out calm vibes. She sure could use some—and her brother could, too. Ty was just like their father: he hated change, especially when it came to their corner of Arizona. Every stranger, every new face was a cause for suspicion. And in some ways, he was right. Even when things on the ranch ran smoothly, the outside world didn't cease to pose a threat. There was always one danger or another lurking out there. They'd had to fight off rogue shifters twice in recent years, not to mention a vampire intrusion. Tension with rival packs was a constant, too.

She watched prickly pear blur past, waving their thorns in warning. Trouble was always afoot. The only question was where it would come from next.

"Damn that old bat and her will," Ty continued.

"Ty!" That, she wouldn't stand for. "Mrs. Seymour was a sweet woman. Don't you ever forget how nice she was to us!"

Ty clenched his jaw and wobbled it right, then left—the closest he ever came to retracting his own words. His gaze, though, went softer. He had to remember the home-baked cookies, the Thanksgiving feasts. Or at least, the couple of feasts their father had let them attend before he decided to slam the door shut. Mrs. Seymour had given them a little taste of normalcy, especially after their mother had taken off. She'd always had a gentle smile and soft words for the Hawthorne kids. For everyone, actually.

"Damn her will, then," Ty muttered.

That, she had to give him. Although Lucy Seymour had passed away several years ago, there were still surprises popping out of her will—or rather, her wills. Because an addendum to the original had recently surfaced. The lawyers had gone over it with a fine-tooth comb and declared it legit. Unusual, but legit.

"Secret heir?" Ty scowled. "What was she thinking?"

"She must have had her reasons." Although for the life of her, Tina couldn't think why Lucy Seymour would leave everything to a secret heir. The rumor mill was rife with speculation on who that might be, since the Seymours had been childless. An illegitimate son, maybe? An old friend? A former lover?

Whoever it was, he or she was keeping a low profile, letting lawyers and the new manager—a person also specified in the will—handle things for now.

"Damn thing, bringing in a new manager out of nowhere," Ty grunted.

"It is odd." Dale Gordon had been foreman of Seymour Ranch for decades. He'd run things capably enough in the period of limbo that followed Lucy Seymour's death. Why rock the boat now? "I bet Dale is delighted."

Ty snorted. "I bet."

She sighed. "Look, we'll be there in another mile. And, who knows? Maybe we'll find out the new manager isn't such a bad guy."

2

"Right."

Dale Gordon was no saint, but he was a known entity, while the new manager was not. And in Ty's mind, a man was guilty until proven innocent.

He did, however, stop scratching his ear long enough to snag one of the cookies Tina held on a plate in her lap.

"Hey!" She slapped at her brother's hand. "Those are for the new manager. Our new neighbor."

"Perfectly good cookies..."

"We're showing that we're friendly."

Ty's scowl etched deep lines on his weathered face.

"You look just like Dad when you do that," she murmured.

He scowled deeper then went through a series of facial contortions to adopt a look of ferocious displeasure that was uniquely his own. Tina held back a chuckle. Her older brother had spent his entire childhood wanting to be a big, bad alpha just like their father, only to realize he wanted to be nothing like the old man at all. He'd softened up a little, Ty had, letting out a little more human and less wolf. Mating had been good for him. Parenthood, too. Tina sent out a silent thanks to whatever fate had paired her brother with a woman like Lana.

Ty waved the cookie in the direction of Seymour Ranch, then shoved it in his mouth. "You planning on buttering the guy up?"

If the front bench of the truck hadn't been so wide, she'd have jabbed an elbow into his ribs. "Definitely not. And it could be a woman for all we know."

Five years ago, Ty might have laughed that comment away, but now he knew better. Another thing he'd learned from his more-than-capable mate.

They drove on in silence. Ty took the last two turns and slowed to coast under the double S brand hanging from the Seymour Ranch gate, then pulled to a halt in front of the homestead. A tall figure separated itself from the shadows of the porch and stepped into the sunlight to greet them.

Tina blinked and bit back a gasp.

The new manager was no woman.

The new manager was no stranger.
The new manager was... *Christ, not him.*

Chapter Two

Tina brought her hands to her eyes, then peeked out, but even that couldn't shake reality away. It really was *him*, in the flesh and raging-hot blood. That easy smile, that athletic frame were unmistakable.

She told herself to straighten her shoulders and pretend there was nothing to notice, nothing to remember. But who was she kidding? Rick was back and her body and soul were already singing for his touch.

"Coming?" Ty grumbled, shoving his door open.

She slid out slowly, holding the plate of cookies before her like a shield. Knowing damn well she'd never find any form of defense against the appeal of this particular man.

The Seymour Ranch manager strode over with the easy, fluid movement of an athlete in his prime. Flannel stretched wide over shoulders rounded with muscle. The checkered pattern across his broad chest led to a waistline that promised rippled abs. He stood balanced on the balls of his feet, at ease yet ready for anything.

Her brother offered him a stiff hand and a glare. "Ty Hawthorne."

Rick didn't blink, nor did he wince at the squeeze Ty must have been hiding in that handshake. His eyes might have been more guarded than she remembered, but the easy, honest smile was the same.

"I remember," he said, nodding. "I'm Rick. Rick Rivera."

Of course he would remember Ty. He'd remember her, too. The question was, how would he see her now? As a passing fancy from foolish days as a youth, or as something more?

Tina stopped breathing when he turned her way. Part of her mind jumped to the memory of the kiss to end all kisses, the night to end all nights. Had that been just another brush of the lips, another ordinary night to a man like him? She could still taste the rich flavor of him. Still feel the sparks shooting through her body. And Christ, that was over a decade ago. That shared night under the stars when they'd lain skin-to-skin, two giddy teenagers flushed with a high of their bodies' own making? Did he remember that as more than just his first time?

Because men moved on from their conquests and didn't look back, right? Especially men who went on to pro baseball careers with million-dollar contracts, as Rick had done. Tina knew; she'd been following his career all along. A little too closely for her own good. The earnest kid from humble beginnings—son of the cook at the ranch next door—had made it to the big leagues.

And now he was back and looking at her with an expression that gave nothing away.

Fast-track careers like his came with a thousand drooling groupies, she knew. And though most of the pictures she'd seen over the years showed Rick swinging in one home run after another, a few photos captured him with eye candy clinging to his arm—women with plunging necklines, silky dresses, and bulging cleavage. How could the memory of a couple sweet nights with a country girl like her compete with that?

Rick's eyes met hers, and her memories rushed into an overwhelming blur, like a landscape seen from a carnival ride. The kind that terrified you, even if you never wanted to get off.

"Tina," he said quietly. The warmth of his hand on hers sent a ripple through her body. "It's been a long time."

Seven years since their last, rushed encounter, and another five back to the time when they'd spent breathless nights together, all summer long. That made twelve long years. Tina knew. She'd counted every day, every night.

Too long, her body sang.

Not long enough, huffed the tiny section of her brain that still worked. Because for all the smoothness in Rick's voice, she could feel a tiny, hopeful tremor in his hand.

He remembered, all right.

The realization rocketed through every nerve in her body, which wasn't a good thing. If he felt the buzz that she'd never forgotten, it would be harder than ever to stay away. Hard to stay away from those earnest, golden-brown eyes that shone with some secret wish she'd never been able to figure out. Hard to keep her fingers from raking through that thick brown hair the way she still did in her dreams.

It would be impossible to say no to this man one more time.

"Hello, Rick," she managed.

In some ways, he hadn't changed a bit: same dimple on the left cheek, same perfect teeth. Time had been good to him. He'd gone from cute rookie to smoking hot pro. His face had an extra line or two, just enough to hint at the depth of character inside. He was only a couple of inches taller than her but easily twice her weight, with most of his bulk in his shoulders and chest—the chest slowly rising and falling, just inches away. She caught her hand sneaking up toward that broad expanse, ready to rest over his heart to feel the beat.

Which, of course, she couldn't do. Not with her brother a foot away. Not with Dale Gordon, the Seymour Ranch foreman, stamping up from behind. Not with her inner wolf wagging its tail like a bitch in heat.

Dale nodded his greeting; Ty grunted back. The cowboys of Arizona had their own brand of charm, and social graces weren't high on their list. Rick was somewhere in between, as he'd always been: a country boy who'd acquired just enough polish without forgetting his roots. The man was one in a million. But she'd known that from the very start.

"You're the new manager," Ty barked.

So much for starting with cookies and a cup of tea.

Tina dragged her eyes from Rick just in time to catch Dale's scowl. Wasn't hard to miss, nor was the slight tightening of Rick's shoulders in response. But Rick's easy expression remained unfazed.

"That's me."

The two men stood eye to eye like a couple of wary steer.

"And what about the owner?" Ty barreled on. "When can I talk to him?"

Most men, Tina figured, would have puffed out their chests and put their own importance on parade. Rick just gave an apologetic shrug. "Sorry, no can do."

He said it with quiet confidence—the kind that came from a man who could admit his mistakes and move on. The eagerness to please had faded, replaced by a firm, take-it-or-leave-it sureness of a man who'd proven himself a thousand times over.

Except when those eyes flicked to hers, there was a gleam that said he had one last thing to prove. Not to Ty or Dale or anyone else. Not to any other woman. Only to her.

Christ, she was a goner. It had taken all she had to turn him down in the past. Twice. There'd been their time together as teens, and that one visit he'd made home in between, when the two of them couldn't resist the temptation to jump into each another's arms yet again. He'd even asked her to go with him when he left.

"Come with me, Tina. Marry me. Be mine."

"I can't." The hoarse whisper she'd barely managed then was on the tip of her tongue now.

Somehow, she'd forced herself to do the right thing back then and say no. She didn't have it in her to do it again.

But now Rick was back and playing to win.

Tina pulled in a long, slow breath. It would be so much easier if she could just tell him. *Rick, you're human, and I'm a shifter. We can't be together. It would never work. The pack needs me, and they'll never accept you.*

Wolves were highly territorial, and Rick, though no shifter, was all alpha male. The leading triad of her pack—her father and her two brothers—would treat Rick like any other intruder if he got too close.

As in, kill him on sight.

Even this little bit of contact with Rick got Ty's wolf riled up. And if she tried bringing Rick home? Forget it.

She shouldn't—couldn't—love Rick. It just couldn't be.

But the mind and the heart were two different things, and hers was long lost to the boy next door.

By the time she worked up the nerve to meet his eyes again, Rick's gaze was back on Ty. "The new owner is a very private man," he said. "I've only ever dealt with the lawyer myself."

"What kind of man doesn't want to run his own ranch?" Ty grumbled, kicking the sand.

Behind Rick, Tina saw Dale spit a wad of tobacco and scowl at Rick. Definitely bad blood there.

Rick shook his head, a small but firm gesture. "I don't know who he is, but I'm sure he wants to maintain good relations with the neighbors."

Ty snorted. "He can start by meeting the neighbors."

Rick gave a tiny shrug, and Tina couldn't help but marvel. Not even her brother could shake him. Of course, standing down one-hundred-mile-an-hour pitches in front of fifty thousand screaming fans probably made for good practice when it came to facing enemy fire.

"And what about the aquifer?" Ty went on, unrelenting.

"The aquifer?" Rich echoed in a totally neutral tone, lobbing the ball straight back into Ty's court.

"Yeah, the aquifer." Ty nodded. "We hear the owner wants to drill deeper and double the output."

Tina waited, watching Rick closely. The water level in the aquifer that fed both Twin Moon and Seymour Ranches was stable, but it would never support higher usage. Rumor had it that the new owner of Seymour Ranch had been inquiring about rights to drill deeper, pump more, and sell the water to the highest bidder. With water being the gold of the modern West... it was a thorny subject, at best.

Rick scratched his chest, looking Ty up and down as if he were speculating where the next curve ball would go.

"I'm not aware that the new owner has plans for any major changes. But don't worry..."

Ty gave him a thorny look that said, *I never do.*

"...I'll make sure you're the first to know as things develop."

In the tense silence that ensued, the grandfather clock inside the house gave a resounding *Bong.* A countdown, Tina sensed, to some uncertain deadline. Things were changing in

Twin Moon's corner of the world. Who knew what trouble they'd have to contend with next?

But surely the boy from next door could be counted on as an ally, not an adversary? She looked at Rick, whose eyes had followed the sound toward the clock. That clock—Lucy Seymour's pride and joy—had fascinated them as kids. They'd invented a dozen stories around it. The clock was haunted, they'd whispered to each other. The clock was a fairy castle. The clock was magic. At night, when the desert was hushed, you could hear the bong from a mile away. Tina knew; she'd crept close sometimes in wolf form just to listen. To hang on to that part of her past.

The part of her past that had Rick in it, too.

His eyes followed the sound, and on the second bong—nine-thirty—his lips gave a tiny quirk, like he was remembering, too.

His mouth opened, closed, then opened again. "Can we talk about this over coffee?"

Tina nodded before thinking. "I brought cookies." Her voice sounded much too hopeful, much too friendly. Even if there was no hope of anything with this man, she couldn't resist.

"Don't think so," Ty grunted, already moving toward the truck and nodding his goodbye to Dale. All Rick got was the smallest tilt of the chin.

Rick gave a polite nod in return. His expression remained unchanged, and he rubbed a slow thumb over his chest, left, then right. Tina ached to reach out and do it for him as she'd once done, so many years ago.

Her eyes met his, and the next second was an eternity. Just the two of them caught in a thousand memories of what once was, of what couldn't possibly be.

God, she'd come so close to running away with him once upon a time.

So why not now? the mournful voice of her soul cried.

Tina leaned in toward the soothing honey brown of his eyes, wondering if the impossible might be possible. Because Rick's full lower lip was pinched between his teeth now, caught in the wistful expression of a boy she knew long ago.

Ty brought the truck to life with a roar, snapping them both back to reality. Tina extended the plate of cookies without breaking Rick's gaze.

"Hope you like them," she whispered over the engine noise.

He smiled and warmth filled her, as if the sun had just risen from behind the hills.

"I know I will." He accepted the cookies with one hand and extended the other. "See you soon?" His fingers gripped hers firmly like, this time, he'd never let her go.

Ty revved the truck, and Rick's eyes jumped over her shoulder, leveling a perfectly steady look at her brother. A one-syllable look that said, *Wait.*

Tina pulled away, suddenly in a hurry. It was one thing for Rick to challenge Ty, man-to-man. But man-to-wolf? He didn't know what he was facing. He had no idea what she was. And if he found out?

The pack guarded its secret fiercely. No one could know.

Not even him.

Chapter Three

Rick stood, watching the pickup scatter gravel in the drive and speed off while Dale stalked away, muttering under his breath.

The minute they were all out of sight, Rick backed up to the top step of the porch and sat down. Hard.

He'd been expecting a visit from the neighbors, but he'd figured it would be old man Hawthorne. He hadn't expected *her*.

He looked down at the plate she'd thrust in his hand, then up to the dust cloud rising over the bluff toward the main road.

Tina Hawthorne. *Dios mio.*

Sweat was just starting to trickle down his face. His heart was revving like he'd just rounded the corner from third to home on a very tight play. A minute longer standing next to her, inhaling that lavender scent of hers, and he'd have lost it completely. Thrown her into a back-bending, knee-rattling kiss, like on an old movie poster. Swung her onto his back and thumped his chest a few times. Gouged the eyes out of Dale Gordon, who'd dare ogle her perfect package of an ass.

Perfect package everything. The perfect curves—not too big, not too small—obvious despite her oversized button-down shirt and plain jeans. The glossy mane of her brown-black hair, the mystery in those midnight eyes that seemed to laugh and cry at the same time.

He scrubbed both hands over his face, feeling the heat in his cheeks. Heat that spread all over as every part of his body reacted in its own love-sick way. His dick fought for space in his jeans, his lungs ached for her return.

Jesus. Tina Hawthorne. Only she could do that to him.

13

He looked up again, and though the dust cloud was settling, his heart rate wasn't. But hell, he didn't need Dale Gordon to see him like this. So he shoved himself to his feet, about-faced into the house, and breezed through the central corridor. Past the grandfather clock and the Seymour family portraits hung on the walls until he emerged on the veranda in the back. Three quick steps across the flagstones to the single step down into the garden, and he sank down again.

How long had it been since he'd seen Tina? Seven years, seven months, and yeah, a couple of days. It had been February first when she rejected him seven years ago. And today was September tenth. So... seven years, seven months, and nine days. He was about to check his watch, because he could probably calculate the minutes, too, but that wasn't good for his sanity. And anyway, a day without her was a day too long.

See you soon? That's what he used to whisper after one of their clandestine meetings as teens.

See you soon. She'd smile and shine and make his heart feel too big for his chest.

He nodded to himself. At least he'd gotten an echo of those words in before her brother had driven her off. *See you soon.*

God, it could never be soon enough.

Tina. She'd been a childhood buddy, then an eye-catching teen, then a gorgeous young woman. She'd always been a class act, but now? Christ, she was out of the ballpark. Somehow, she'd ripened, not aged. Same silky hair that shone in the sun. Same smooth, baby skin. Same fire in her eyes when she looked at him. But something about her said she was older, wiser, more careful now. A little sadder, too, but that only made him want her more. To give her whatever she needed to laugh and smile and glow.

He dug a heel into the gravel. It would have been easier if she'd aged the way so many old friends had: looking wearier, baggier, with a couple of clamoring kids clinging to her clothes. That and a big-ass wedding ring that screamed *Hands off*, plus a husband with a shotgun and a very mean dog.

But there was no ring. No husband. The only ring she wore was a plain one, and on the wrong finger. The guiltless lust that filled her eyes as her lips quivered proved it, too.

No, there were no contenders, except for that overprotective family of hers. The only difference to their early days was that the fire-breathing dragon of a father lurking over her shoulder had been replaced by a fire-breathing dragon of a brother. The one looking at him like he'd never be good enough for Tina. Not as the son of a lowly Latino cook, not even as a ball player. He'd hoped they'd see him differently now that he was back as manager, but it sure didn't seem that way.

In a roundabout way, he owed that cranky, overprotective family of Tina's. They'd kept her safe from the cowboys, the city slickers, the prospectors who must have passed by throughout the years. Because Tina was a true prize. A diamond who didn't know the meaning of rough. A soul mate, just for him.

If only she'd let him in.

Well, he was back now. Back for his third and final chance. If he didn't succeed this time, he'd take it like a man—three strikes and all that—or cry his heart out for twenty days and nights then eventually grow old alone, dreaming about her the way he'd dreamed for the past twelve years.

Either way, he hadn't thought things through that far. Hadn't thought any of this through. There hadn't been time. It had only been a week ago that he learned he'd been named manager of Seymour Ranch. Perfect timing, considering he had still been contemplating how to launch a second career six months after the accident that ended his days in the league.

Of course, he'd always known those days were numbered and planned on a new start. He'd finished business school on the side with that in mind. It had taken him years of part-time study, hammering away whenever work gave him the chance, but he'd finally done it. He'd been getting ready to put that degree to use when an addendum to sweet old Lucy Seymour's will came to light, naming him as manager of this ranch.

So here he was, back where he started. In more ways than one.

He let his eyes drift to the ragged mess that the once-vibrant garden had become. Weeding it was one of the items on his list, along with finding out what the hell this aquifer business was all about. His gaze went from the sun-dried adelias and choked-off gaillardias to the space beyond.

Right over there was the batting cage he and his dad had built. All rusty and overgrown, not like it had been for that *Sports Illustrated* photo shoot his agent had talked him into a couple of years back. Even he had to smile at the story—country kid grown up in isolation becomes baseball star, thanks to a rusty old pitching machine the neighbors didn't want.

His mouth curved into a frown. The neighbors were Dale Gordon and his sons. Old Dale had played a little minor-league ball in his time and had visions of his sons making it big someday. So he'd picked up a discount pitching machine somewhere and set it up. But Dale's two boys had turned to more satisfying hobbies, like shooting beer cans, jackrabbits, or any snake unlucky enough to cross the sights of their BB guns.

So Rick and his dad had bought the machine off Dale. Set it up in a nice, even spot and put up a cage made of cast-off lengths of fence. They couldn't afford new stuff, but they made do.

"Perfect."

He could still remember his father nodding at it with pride.

A sigh built in his chest. Weeding the batting cage would go on his list, too, right after the garden.

"The best batting cage in the world," his dad had said.

And it was, because it was his, and it worked. It was fun. Focusing on the chute, the ball, his swing—that filled the time his dad couldn't color with stories of Rick's mother, who'd died much too young.

Yeah, the pitching machine worked, all right. The lonely kid on the remote ranch had batted his way right into a college scholarship, then into the major leagues. So in a weird way, he owed Dale Gordon and his no-good sons. If it weren't for that pitching machine, he might be like them—a couple of thirty-year-old drifters doing who-knows-what.

Lucky for Rick, he hadn't seen either of Dale's sons since his return. Just Dale—and far too much of him. Lucy Seymour

16

had managed to keep the foreman sober, but these days, he'd taken to hitting the bottle. Hard and often, it seemed.

Rick kicked at the dirt and shook his head. Funny how some dreams panned out and others didn't. And funny how some dreams changed. Used to be, he would line the pitching machine up so he'd face the mesa and pretend it was a stadium full of fans, screaming for a grand slam. But after a year or two of playing major-league ball, he started doing it the other way around. Even in the oldest, most venerated parks like Fenway or Wrigley Field, he'd let his imagination take out the grandstands and crowds and substitute Arizona instead. This space. This peace. This sky.

Home. Home had been calling him for a while.

And now the ghost of Mrs. Seymour had finally brought him back. Back home.

Back to Tina.

They'd played together as kids, then played a different way as teens. Lost their virginity together that magical night in Spring Hollow, and followed that up all summer, sneaking off to clandestine rendezvous once their chores were done. But then a talent scout had come along and made Rick an offer too good to resist. One thing led to another, and Rick ended up in college, and eventually, the big leagues. It all went so fast, and he had nearly convinced himself that what he and Tina had was just a kid thing. Puppy love, right?

But puppy love didn't last over twelve years and a thousand miles. Puppy love didn't propel a man and a woman right back into each other's arms the minute they laid eyes on each other when he finally did visit home.

Home. Arizona. Tina. He sighed, remembering it all.

That week they'd shared seven years ago had been a whirl-wind of passion and burning need. No giggles, only intense gazes as if the end of the week signaled the end of the world. And it did, in a way.

"Come with me," he'd urged her when the week was up. "Come to California. Marry me." She'd barely left the ranch in all those years, and he was just what she needed—a knight in shining armor to carry her away. "Be mine."

He remembered how her eyes had blazed with hope, then dimmed to twin shadows before she forced a bittersweet smile. "I can't, Rick." No explanation, though he sensed a cascade of words poised on her tongue. She looked at him with those weepy eyes, so full of secrets.

Why? He wanted to plead. *Why?*

"I just can't," she whispered. Seven long years ago.

He took a deep breath, then another. When a raven cawed, his gaze snapped up from wherever it had drifted to and focused back on the overgrown garden.

Tina. Love. Last chances. He could spend all day staring into the wind, thinking about it. But he had a ranch to run, and an awfully fine line to walk between old ways and new— not to mention a bitter old man as a foreman and neighbors who expected the worst.

Rick sucked in a long, slow breath. He'd take it one day at a time with Tina and with the ranch. Lucy Seymour's husband, Henry, used to say the first twenty days of anything were the worst, and Rick had used that as a benchmark throughout his life. His first miserable twenty days away from home back when he was a teen. His first grueling twenty days in the big leagues. The first hopeless twenty in the hospital.

And now this. His first twenty days on the ranch.

His hand balled into a fist, but something got in his way. The cookie plate. He looked down and studied it for a minute. Chocolate chunk cookies, by the look of it, lumpy as the surface of the moon and just starting to melt in the sunshine. Perfect.

He bit into one and let the flavor explode in his mouth. Pictured Tina holding the bowl at her hip, mixing the batter. Wiping a smear with her finger, then extending it to him.

He sucked in a sharp breath when the next image popped into his mind, all by itself. He was just leaning over to lick that finger when a tiny Tina look-alike came pattering along, giggling, *Daddy, Daddy,* and got to it first.

Now, shoot. Did his imagination really have to torture him like that?

He closed his eyes and held on to that picture for a good, long time.

The next cookie, he held up to the hills in a silent toast to their maker—and to twenty days.

Chapter Four

Tina's head buzzed all the way home.

Other body parts, too. Her face tingled like she'd gotten too much sun. Her stomach fluttered. Heat pooled low in her body and slid around in slow, sultry waves.

Ty slapped the steering wheel as he drove. "Can you believe it?"

No, she couldn't. Destiny had made a terrible mistake, letting her meet Rick all those years ago. Letting her soar with hope then crash brutally to the ground because her destined mate was human. Female shifters couldn't mate with humans for good reason, so it was either one big mistake, or one awful trick of fate. She'd given up on love years ago, because if she couldn't have Rick, she didn't want anyone.

And now he was back. Worse, as manager of Seymour Ranch! She'd have to deal with him regularly. She could practically hear the cruel laugh of destiny on the sidelines, witnessing the torture that every business meeting with him would be. She'd be able to see her true love but not touch him or hold him or kiss him or—

"Fucking unbelievable," Ty went on.

Tina gave a bitter nod as her eyes tracked the landscape outside. The desert seemed drier, more withered than it had before. The cactus graying, the brushwood drooping.

The pickup rattled over a series of cattle grids and then under the Twin Moon Ranch gate. Overhead, even the ranch brand seemed to mock her: two circles, overlapping by one-third. A perfect representation of her and Rick. Two lovers connected in their hearts, yet forever pulled apart.

"And now this," Ty muttered.

She could have listed a dozen things about Rick that could have qualified as *this*, but Ty was waving at the first building on the right where several concerned faces stood in an expectant huddle.

"Trouble," he growled.

Trouble for sure, she nodded, still thinking about Rick.

Ty parked, slammed the door, and stalked to the meeting house. Tina followed on feet that felt heavier, older than before. She climbed the three steps to the shaded porch, followed Ty in, and gave her younger brother Cody a nod of greeting.

Normally, she would have whisked straight to her usual spot—the chair beside her father's empty seat. But she paused just inside the door. So much had changed in the past years, and yet everything was the same. Her father, the retired alpha, was away, helping a leaderless wolfpack in Colorado, and Ty and Cody were leading in his place. But she was still Good Old Tina. Still alone.

"So, how did it go?" Cody smiled.

"How do you think it went?" Ty grumbled.

Ah, her dear brothers: one was pure sunshine, the other, a thundercloud. Between the two of them, they made a great team.

A leadership team Tina was part of, too. Their father had never taken a mate, so she'd served as de facto alpha female for years. Good Old Tina, working quietly in the wings. Good Old Tina, smoothing over her brothers' rougher edges.

Good Old Tina, destined to fill the same role for the rest of her life.

"So tell us, already!" Lana insisted.

Tina breathed a sigh of relief. Ty's mate had a calming influence on him. Just for that, Lana was a welcome addition to the pack. As an expert in land rights, she was a double win.

Tina returned Lana's bolstering smile. That was the other great thing about Lana: she was a friend, too. The only other woman this close to the heart of the pack. The only one who truly understood the pressure Tina faced.

If only Lana weren't so damn good at everything. Because she'd all but put Tina out of a job. In a way, that was great.

Tina finally had time to concentrate on her official job as ranch accountant, and she finally had time for herself. The problem was, she'd quickly run out of things to do with that time. There was only so much fixing her cute little bungalow needed, so much gardening to do, so many books to read. Without a mate or kids...

Tina stood a little straighter and told herself not to sink into that morass. She had nieces and a nephew to smother in love. Packmates to support. Cookies to bake.

Cookies. Her thoughts snagged there. Did Rick like chocolate chunk?

"Rick." His name slipped out of her mouth, and everyone's attention jumped to her. "Rick Rivera." She quickly covered up. "He's the new manager of Seymour Ranch."

"Rick Rivera—that Rick?" Cody asked, rubbing a thumb over his chest in a perfect imitation of Rick's little gesture.

Lana's eyes went wide. "Rick Rivera—that Rick?" She swung an imaginary bat.

Tina let out a weary sigh. "That Rick." If only they knew.

"He always seemed like a good enough guy," Cody started. "And if the Seymours trust him enough to make him manager—"

"I don't trust him," Ty growled.

"You don't trust anyone," Lana sighed.

Ty changed tacks. "He wouldn't tell us who the new owner is."

Tina cut in there. "He doesn't know." A hidden growl tickled the back of her throat—her inner wolf, grumbling in Rick's defense. Which was crazy, since her wolf should be loyal to her pack, not to a man she couldn't have.

The growl deepened until Tina forced it away with a cough.

"He *claims* he doesn't know. And he wouldn't talk about the aquifer," Ty fumed. He turned to Lana and all eyes followed. "What do you think?"

"Hard to tell. My contact at Water Resources tipped me off that someone's been asking around about how to file a petition to drill deeper and double the output from the Cameron aquifer."

Tina stiffened. The Cameron aquifer only ran under two properties—Twin Moon and Seymour Ranch.

"And since it wasn't us putting in the request..." Cody started.

"It has to be him," Ty growled.

Lana put her hands up in caution. "So far, nothing has been filed."

"And what if they do?" Tina asked, careful to refer to use a more neutral *they* than a specific *he*. "What are the chances of it getting approved?"

"Conservation laws are dead against it, but you know how it goes. Money talks, and they keep finding loopholes to keep pumping water." Lana scowled. "No foresight whatsoever."

"Could the aquifer support more use?"

"Absolutely not. We're at the limit right now, and that's with us following all of Stef's recommendations on recharge and conservation."

Tina nodded. Stef was a relative newcomer to Twin Moon Ranch and another valuable asset with her renewable resources expertise. Bit by bit, the pack had developed a top-notch team, to the point that other packs came seeking their advice. In the old days, the wolfpacks of the West had vied for status on the virtue of their physical strength. Nowadays, Twin Moon paired that with brains and knowledge. They'd need all the advantages they could get, though, to face the challenges ahead.

"Can't we get any more information out of that contact of yours?" Ty asked.

"Nope," Lana said with a firm shake of the head. "So far, it's all just vague—"

A fist thumped on the door, and Zack stepped in, his forehead lined with worry. The woman following him—his mate, Rae—looked just as anxious, and not about the repercussions of interrupting a meeting. Those two were among a handful of pack members with high enough standing to get away with it.

"Sorry," Zack said. "But we got trouble, Ty."

Tina winced at the words. Didn't they already have enough trouble?

Chapter Five

"The coyote pack has reports of—" Zack started, then broke off sharply, looking around as if he'd already let too much slip.

Tina stiffened. Zack was the pack's best tracker. For him and Rae, a skilled hunter, to look so concerned meant there had to be some kind of intruder on the prowl. One powerful enough to pose a serious risk to the packs.

"Atsa's on his way," Zack said. His voice was studiously even, his face grave.

Atsa, the ruling coyote elder from the neighboring pack to the west? The aging Navajo leader rarely left home territory, and never for social calls.

"Atsa is coming here?" Tina blurted.

"Now." Zack nodded.

Two dusty pickups pulled up outside, and all eyes peered through a window as the white-haired elder eased out of one and made his way toward the council house. His steps were cautious but dignified, and heavy with concern.

Tina glanced at Ty in time to see Lana sliding a gentle hand down his cheek. The lines of Ty's face eased into the briefest of smiles as he leaned closer to his mate. It was one of those moments when the space around them almost seemed to glow, and Tina was suspended between wanting to watch and the urge to turn her back. That sureness, that trust. That you-and-I-can-conquer-all… What she wouldn't give to have a partnership like that.

And just like that, her thoughts boomeranged back to Rick. Rick, with his earnest eyes and easy smile. Rick, with his magical touch. Rick, with the soft voice, asking her to leave everything and follow him.

Rick, forcing an understanding smile when she'd turned him down.

Ty strode to the door to meet Atsa outside in the ultimate sign of respect between ruling alphas. Zack and Rae stepped forward, too, exuding the badass hunter vibe they did so well. Between those two and Tina's other packmates, Twin Moon pack could easily deal with whatever trouble Atsa was coming to report. Right?

That's what Tina wanted to believe, but her wolf was pacing inside, rumbling in concern. The last time Atsa had visited, it was to warn them about a band of coyote rogues. What danger was lurking in the desert now?

All eyes swung to the entrance, then flicked downward in a sign of respect as Ty held the door open for Atsa. The coyote elder had always seemed ancient to Tina, even when she was a kid. But now he was even older. Wiser. And definitely concerned.

When Tina looked up again, Atsa nodded to Ty. The room practically hummed with their power. Two alphas at opposite ends of their reigns. One, the wise old alpha; the other, a powerful young gun.

"Our allied packs have faced many challenges over the years," Atsa started.

Tina found herself nodding warily. Not a promising overture. The coyote-shifter Navajos had proven to be loyal allies again and again. They needed each other, Twin Moon and Echo Creek packs, to guard their secrets from the human world.

"I fear we have a new challenge now."

Tina held her breath, as did everyone else in the room. What was it this time? Rogues? Vampires? Power-hungry shifters from the north? They'd faced all those enemies in recent years, and each time come out ahead, if barely alive. The faces around her were grim.

"Our cousins in the eastern part of the state report a disturbance."

Ty lifted an eyebrow.

"A demon awakened," Atsa whispered, and the room went still. So still Tina could hear the quiet swish of a pine bough over the roof.

"Demon?" Ty's harsh voice broke the silence a moment later. "What kind?"

Tina exchanged glances with Lana. There were demons of all kinds, and none were easy to destroy.

Atsa swallowed, and when he spoke again, his ancient voice was a whisper. "Hellhound."

A shiver ran down Tina's spine. Zack and Rae exchanged knowing glances, and even Ty went stiff.

"Where?" he demanded. "How sure are you?"

Zack shot Ty a sharp look that said, *Atsa wouldn't be here if he wasn't sure.*

The Navajo elder tilted his head left then right. "We have a report from two hundred miles east. Until now, the sightings have been unconfirmed. Red eyes in the night, howling from deep inside the earth."

Tina shivered. A ghost story come to life. But was it really true?

"Red eyes and noises could be anything," Cody pointed out.

Atsa nodded. "That was what we thought, until. . . "

He trailed off and let the next seconds stretch into a minute. A full, quiet minute in which Tina counted the beats of her racing heart.

"Until?" Ty barked.

"Until the sightings stopped. At the same time, our shaman had a vision of a hellhound, pacing an underground cavern. Looking for some means of escape. Looking for an exit to our world." Atsa paused again and closed his eyes. "Finding one."

Tina's heart stuttered, then thumped on. *Finding a way out?*

"Our shaman saw a vision through the hellhound's eyes. A tunnel, a flickering light. A man's voice, calling in pain. And then a view." Atsa's arms swept over toward the windows. "This view. Our view. Bitterroot Valley."

27

Chapter Six

The council house went quiet and stayed that way long after Atsa left. Having said his piece, the old man looked fragile and worn as he leaned on the arm of the grandson who helped him outside.

Tina, like the others, watched Atsa make his way to his truck. Watched Ty walk alongside, and then stand for a long time, observing the dust rise then settle in the wake of the pickup before stalking back inside. He thumped four steps across the room, sank into a chair, and ran a hand through his brown-black hair.

Even then it was silent, everyone submerged in their own fears.

"Hellhound?" Lana ventured at last. Tina looked up to see her sister-in-law's eyes skip across the room. There was a hopeful note in Lana's voice. Hoping, perhaps, that the threat wasn't so grave. "Back on the East Coast, we've had the occasional demon. Well, more like stories of demons, like my grandfather used to tell. But never a hellhound."

Tina glanced around the room, then took a deep breath. "There hasn't been one in generations. But according to the stories..." She swung her gaze toward the windows, in the direction Atsa had indicated.

"What do they say?" Lana prompted.

Tina told herself that talking about the old stories wasn't the same as believing them. "Like Atsa said. They come from the bowels of the earth."

"From hell," Cody added. "Old-time miners used to tell stories about red eyes and ghostly howls from the inside of the earth."

"Creatures bound to the underworld," Tina continued. "But sometimes, they get..."

"Unleashed," Lana whispered in the same grim tone Atsa had used.

Tina nodded. "Then they come looking for a way out. To our world."

A long, contemplative silence set in while Tina's mind filled in the blanks. Her skin broke out in goose bumps just imagining it.

"And then?" Lana asked.

Tina took a deep breath before answering. "They kill."

"And kill," Cody added.

"And kill," Ty said, looking ready to tear the beast to pieces if it ventured onto his territory. But it wasn't that easy. Tina knew that as well as Ty did.

"How do you get rid of one?" Lana's voice remained steady, but worry flared in her eyes.

Tina saw her brothers exchange grim looks and then turn to Zack with something like hope. Maybe their half-coyote packmate could search his Navajo heritage to find some handy trick for destroying a hellhound.

Zack shook his head slowly, not quite a no, not quite a yes. "You tear it apart," he said in a gritty, determined voice. "You get every wolf in the county together. Gather your allies..."

Tina's mind raced. Who could they call on, other than the coyotes? "Westend pack, maybe?"

Everyone rolled their eyes.

"Just try prying them away from their casinos," Rae snorted.

Tina saw Lana's flit to Ty's. "What about the javelinas?"

Twin Moon pack had recently renewed an alliance with a clan of shapeshifting boars. Massive wild pigs, as Lana had described them after a brief encounter, years ago.

Ty shook his head. "Good luck finding them."

"There were those cougars..." Lana murmured, looking at Rae.

"But who knows where they are by now?" Rae said.

The room went silent.

"All right." Tina tried sounding upbeat. "Us and the coyotes, then. What do we need to do to kill a hellhound?"

Zack pursed his lips, considering. "You attack it from all sides. Hope it doesn't kill too many of you while you try to kill it."

"Try?" Ty demanded, his voice harsh, unsatisfied.

"Try." Zack stared right back.

They glared at each other until Lana butted in, waving her hand to dissipate the tension in the room. "How reliable is Atsa's shaman?"

Just what Tina had been wondering herself.

"He's had visions that are dead-on and others that never amount to anything." Tina racked her memory, weighing up the shaman's track record. "Mostly, he's so vague, you can never be sure."

"Sounds like a horoscope," Lana muttered.

Tina had to smile. "Yeah, a little like that. Sometimes nothing comes of his ramblings. But other times..." She paused, remembering the exceptions. "Sometimes he's right on the mark. Uncannily so. Like the time the pump house burned down."

Cody nodded. "Like the flash flood a couple of years ago."

Zack kicked at the floorboards. "Like the skinwalker troubles over in Weston when we were kids."

Tina let her mind roam beyond the walls of the council house. She pictured the mighty cottonwoods, casting cool shade over the roof. The peaceful scattering of homes. The rocky bluffs in the distance, standing sentinel as they had for eons.

Security was an illusion. Peace, a fleeting thing. Trouble was always lurking somewhere. It was especially true in the desert, with its wrinkled hills and banded cliffs. With every fiery sunset, the red rocks whispered warnings, even as the purple mountains in the distance tried to soothe. There was beauty; there was danger. They were intertwined, like two separate strands making up a single thread.

Ty cleared his throat sharply. "Double the guard."

31

"Got it." Cody nodded, heading out. He'd rustle up every pack member capable of standing a good watch, Tina figured, then head straight over to check on the schoolhouse and his mate.

Ty turned to Zack and Rae. "You two good to head out?"

Tina watched the couple's eyes meet and exchange a thousand devoted vows that said they'd fight to the death for each other and for the ranch.

"We're on it," Zack said, following Rae outside.

Which left Ty and Lana staring into each other's eyes and Tina standing quietly on the side.

She tucked her upper lip under the lower and headed out silently. Good Old Tina. Unnoticed. Alone.

Chapter Seven

Rick spent the morning shoveling papers from one side of Henry Seymour's desk to the other, trying to settle his mind on one thing. Anything. Water rights. Inventory. Deductible business losses. Anything but Tina.

He kept wandering out on the porch, though, looking toward the north. Toward Twin Moon Ranch.

Funny folk, they are.

He remembered standing there after a Thanksgiving feast, years ago, watching Tina and her family head over the hill. The Hawthornes had been invited every year, but they'd only come a few times. He remembered meeting Tina's mother, that first year the Hawthornes had come over. Everyone had been sadder and quieter the second year. Angrier, the third. Distant, the fourth.

There was no fifth year, because the neighbor kids quit coming. But he and Tina still saw each other whenever they could.

He remembered it exactly, right down to Henry Seymour standing on the porch saying, *Funny folk, they are.*

Good, hardworking folk, Lucy Seymour had replied.

Rick remembered turning to look up at her. Her smiling face was a long way up back then, because he had been just a kid.

Good folk, all right, Henry had agreed. *But there's something different about them.*

Rick couldn't agree more. There'd always been something different about the Hawthorne clan. About the whole of Twin Moon Ranch. The way they kept to themselves. The way they moved, even: smooth and silent, like so many hunters on the prowl. The way they eyed the horizon and sniffed, like they could scent the onset of night.

We're all human, Lucy Seymour would say then pat her husband's arm. *We all do our best.*

Rick remembered his dad standing by his shoulder and giving it an encouraging squeeze. *We all do our best,* he'd echo, smiling so broadly, Rick knew his dad meant him. Doing his best.

Once upon a time, that meant sweeping up the kitchen and helping out around the ranch. Then doing his best had become slugging balls right out of the park. And now... His eyes swept across the view. The brown, undulating hills, the patches of prickly pear bursting with wine-red bulbs. Now he'd do his best with the ranch. He owed it to the Seymours, who'd treated him like one of their own.

His gaze drifted to the little rise to the west. Up there was the cemetery where four generations of Seymours were buried. Rick's parents were buried there, too.

His mom—he could smile, thinking about her. He'd had enough time to get used to the idea that she was gone. But his dad... He frowned. He'd never get used to that, even with a year gone by. Would never accept the way a good man's life came to a shattering end.

And just like that, before he could even think about what he was doing, Rick was in his truck and heading out the back road to Dead Horse Bluff. A fitting name, though it wasn't only horses that died up there.

He drove up the long rise, glancing at the wall of purple mountains on the horizon. At the crest of the hill, the whole of Bitterroot Valley spread before him, miles wide. A broad, pocked valley with a ribbon of green at its heart. Most times of year, the creek was only a trickle, but that was enough to nurture a thin strip of life. He coasted down a dip then revved up again, following a bend up the snaking track toward the back of the mesa until he was there at the bluffs. Three miles as the crow flies, twelve by road.

What the hell had brought his father out to Dead Horse Bluff that day?

Rick slid out of the truck and kicked at the dirt. The breathtaking beauty of the Arizona desert had skipped over this dusty place. It was dull and listless. Lifeless. The wind blew stronger here. Meaner.

Over to the right, backed into a fold of the hill, stood the boarded-over entrance to the old Diablo Mine. A place his dad had warned him away from a hundred times—the only time he could remember his father's kind features turning fierce.

Never go near there, you understand? It's a bad, bad place.

For years, that had been enough—that, and the fear tingeing his father's voice, plus the stories Dale Gordon's boys scared him with. Ghost stories in which miners went in but never came out. Men going mad from whatever it was they'd seen or heard at the gateway to hell.

Rick had never gone near the mine. Never even been tempted to peek behind the boards closing up the shaft. The police report hadn't made any mention of the mine, so he walked straight to the edge of the cliff, a hundred feet farther along.

He peered down, swallowing away the lump in his throat. His father had fallen down that?

It was a place where Mother Nature had gotten fed up and started over, like an artist crying in frustration and tearing up a half-finished work. That's just what it looked like: a jagged tear in the landscape where one level petered out into open air while the other slid in, ten stories below. The end of the earth.

A raven cawed, and the sound carried on the wind.

He stood there a while, leaning over the edge, letting the hot desert air pull at his shirt and his hair. Wondering what it would feel like in the startling moments between a foothold up here and a crashing end down there.

Wondering why. How. How could his father have died here at the end of the earth?

"The end of the line," a voice said, too loud and too close.

Rick jolted and barely jerked back from stumbling off the cliff. He spun to see Dale Gordon standing right beside him, wearing a satisfied grin.

Rick was that close to wiping the smile off Dale's face when he caught himself. *Cool, stay cool.* Just like at bat. Don't let his surprise show, no matter how jittery his insides were.

"Dale," he muttered, keeping his voice flat. Why was Dale sneaking up on him here, of all places? He blinked, and something inside him sank.

It was his eye. That was it. The eye damaged in the accident. Dale hadn't been sneaking up; it was only that Rick had no peripheral vision on that side.

"Howdy, hotshot," Dale replied, sending a wave of whiskey-scented breath Rick's way.

He held back the grimace—at the odor, at the nickname. Maybe even at the man. Dale Gordon used to be a man he could respect. A man the Seymours trusted. A man who did his job and mostly left everyone else alone. But somewhere along the line, he'd taken a sharp downhill turn.

Dale leaned out and gave the precipice an appraising look. "Real shame about your father," he muttered. "Unlucky."

The way he said it invited Rick to wonder if luck—good or bad—had anything to do with his father's death. He narrowed his gaze to Dale's bloodshot eyes and found innocence. Sweet, insistent innocence.

That his father's death might not have been an accident had crossed his mind before, even though the police report insisted there'd been no sign of foul play. There was no reason to believe anyone would target Jorge Rivera, the amiable ranch cook everybody liked. A nobody.

The sweetest, kindest nobody who'd ever lived.

Rick gulped, refusing to blink as Dale stared back. The dark, darting eyes dared Rick to speculate. How would Dale stand to benefit from his father's death?

He glanced over Dale's shoulder and saw the man's red truck parked right beside his.

See? The front grill seemed to grin. *No sneaking up. Just parked here, very innocently.*

He was probably just being touchy. Jumpy, because of his bad eye. Seeing Tina that morning had turned him upside down too, and coming here had given his heart an extra shake.

He stepped away from the cliff's edge. Away from the last place his father drew a lungful of air before meeting a horrible end. Wondering why. His father hadn't given any hint of being lonely or afraid, not the last time they'd met, a month before his death. Not ever, in fact, because his dad was a fountain of sunshine. The type to smile and celebrate every memory of a beloved wife rather than mourn his loss. The type to look a problem in the eye and smile or sing it away.

Not the type to wander too close to the edge of a cliff and slip, and certainly not the type to jump, as the police report suggested.

"What are you doing up here?" Rick asked, changing the subject. Keeping his hands balled into fists at his sides because there was no reason, no reason at all to swipe at the itch around his eyes.

"Been boarding the mine up," Dale replied, striding along at Rick's side. His blind side, damn him.

Rick glanced at the entrance without heading over. Boarding it up? It looked more like someone had been prying it open.

"Keeping it safe," Dale said. The word sounded forced coming from his lips. "You know, from any wandering kids."

"Right." Like any kid would come wandering up here.

Rick didn't nod as he said it. Didn't put any conviction in his reply. He just stood and stared at Dale the way he'd stare down a pitcher. A pitcher with dirt in his pockets and tricks up his sleeve. A pitcher who'd stop at nothing to win.

Rick stared. Okay, maybe glared. Glared and wondered about cooks and cliffs and bitter old men until Dale coughed and turned away.

Rick climbed into the cab of his truck, slammed the door, and fired the engine up into an angry roar. He headed back to the ranch, clenching the steering wheel so hard, his knuckles showed white.

Keeping it safe, Dale claimed.

Rick swallowed down the bitter taste in his mouth. Right.

Chapter Eight

Three days passed. Three days Tina spent in a flurry of cleaning that included pulling down half the decorations wallpapering her refrigerator—the half that were newspaper and magazine clippings about Rick. Down with the newspaper article about the last batting record he'd set. Down with the one that chronicled his injury. Down with the season schedule for the San Diego Padres. Maybe if she pulled them all down, the ache would go away.

Those were the days. The nights, she'd spent alternating between nightmares of demon incursions and sweet, sultry dreams of Rick. With each passing day, though, the nightmares receded and the dreams dominated.

Dreams of touching him. Holding him. Kissing his ear. Feeling his breath on her cheek as his fingers intertwined with hers. Some of the images stemmed from memories, others pure fantasy. His lips would reach for hers and kiss her, soft and sweet. Then longer and harder as their bodies inched closer and her fists tightened on his shirt. He'd pull her into a hug and hold her like a man determined to never, ever let go—except maybe to let her step back and lead him to the bedroom of her little bungalow, where he'd undress her slowly, reverently, then lower her to the bed. Settle his weight over her body and murmur how beautiful she was. His eyes would flash as he ran a finger along her collarbone and—

"Nothing yet."

Tina snapped out of her daydream and blinked at Ty, coming in the door of his office. She'd been so desperate for distraction, she'd been tidying his space, too. What she really needed to tidy was her mind before her brother caught her thoughts. One of the drawbacks of shifter telepathy.

"No sign?" she managed, hastily wiping the image of Rick out of her mind. Well, trying to.

"Not a thing," Ty growled. His eyes burned with frustration. "We've been all over the valley—and into the next, and the next—and can't find a trace of demon anywhere."

Tina nodded. She'd put in her hours, too, trotting to the far reaches of the ranch in wolf form, searching for the peppery scent of demon. Finding nothing.

"Maybe that's a good thing," she ventured.

"Right," Ty grumbled.

Lana loped in after him with an apologetic nod and started on a neck massage of her mate. "If it's out there, we'll find it," she said. "But you need some rest, my love."

Ty's eyelids drooped as his mate's touch worked its magic. Lana glanced at Tina with a wink.

Thank God for her brother's mate. The growls of anger quickly subsided as Tina made her exit, knowing where that massage would end. As in, hot and heavy on the desk in their own form of deep tissue massage.

She sighed and walked to her own office, eyeing the silent, empty space from the doorway before sagging to her chair. She swiveled in a slow circle, staring at the walls. Good Old Tina, doing what she did best. Working. Wishing.

Alone.

"Heya, Tina."

Cody sauntered through the door. Her younger brother plonked down on the couch and scraped his fingers through his hair.

"I guess you haven't found anything, either."

"Nothing." Cody sighed, leaned back, and looked at the ceiling. "I'm starting to wonder if there really is a hellhound. I don't know what's worse, getting—"

He bolted upright a split second before the sound of a high-pitched wail came through the door.

"Daddy! Daddy!" the voice cried, and two figures appeared at the door. Cody's mate Heather, with baby Sammie on her hip, and their older daughter Holly.

"Minor crisis," Heather murmured as Holly threw herself into Cody's arms.

"Daaaaaddy!" she wailed.

"What is it, Muffin?"

Tina couldn't help smiling despite her niece's tears. Watching Cody comfort Holly, hold her close while Heather checked the sleepy baby... Tina and her siblings might not have experienced that kind of unabashed love as kids, but it was good to see the next generation receive their due. Funny, though, that it just made the ache in her worse.

"Pinkie died!" Holly wailed on.

"Oh, sweetie, that's so sad." Cody lifted an eyebrow at Tina over his daughter's shoulder. *We're worried about hellhounds; she's worried about her pet fish.* He sent the comment straight into her mind along with an exaggerated sigh.

Tina gave him a crooked smile. *Good. Let her tragedies be small ones.*

Heather came closer to slide a hand over Cody's back, and he lit up like a Christmas tree. He caught Heather's hand without looking and squeezed, turning the light on in her, too. Tina blinked at the two of them. So sweet. So painfully sweet to see.

"But Muffin, I think Pinkie was old," Cody said.

"That's what Mommy says. Mommy says Pinkie is going to heaven. But Greenie will be alone." Holly sniffed. "He'll be so sad."

Tina drew in a deep breath. She knew all about being alone.

"So let's get Greenie a new friend, then," Cody said.

Tina sighed. If only finding good company was that easy. Company she wanted. Company she loved. Her gaze wandered south, toward Seymour Ranch.

"But Mommy says she can't go to town today. Greenie might die if we wait!"

"Pumpkin, I think Greenie can wait a day."

"He can't! He can't!"

Tina watched Cody and Heather exchange tight looks, on the cusp of deciding. Giving in might be edging too close to spoiling their daughter, something Heather just wouldn't stand for.

But Tina, as auntie, could spoil her niece all she wanted. She squatted down by Holly. "I can get Greenie a friend when I go to town."

Holly's head popped up, making blond locks cascade across her narrow shoulders. "Today?"

Tina hadn't been planning on going until tomorrow, but...

"Yes, I'm going right away."

Two little arms caught her in a neck hug and hung on tight. Tina held on, too, rocking her niece. Sniffed her baby-shampoo-and-buttercup scent. Marveled at the miracle of life one more time and winced at the ache that came with it. That yearning to make a miracle of her own.

"What do you say?" Heather and Cody prompted in unison when Holly finally emerged from her hug.

"Thank you! Thank you!" Holly gushed.

"You don't have to go, you know," Heather said, peeling Holly away.

"No, it's fine. I wanted to get some errands done before Carly arrives."

"Auntie Carly is coming?" Holly clapped her hands. "From California? Soon?"

"Yes, soon." Cody looked at Tina with a *Yeah, brace yourself* kind of look. Tina knew just what he meant. Their younger sister had a style and temperament all her own.

"Well, I better get going, then," Tina said. "Does Greenie want a pink friend or a different color friend?"

"Any color," Holly said. "Just a friend."

The words played through her mind on the forty-five minute drive to town and all through the aisles of the feed and hardware store. A friend. Just a friend. Was that so much to ask?

She made her way back out to the parking lot with a silver-blue fish in a baggie of water in one hand, a package of tulip bulbs clutched under her elbow, and a forty-pound sack of horse feed hoisted over her shoulder. The balancing act would have worked, too, if her purse strap hadn't slipped off. When it did, the jolt on her arm made her drop the keys to her old Corolla.

"Shit," she muttered and kneeled, fishing for the keys. Leaning right to keep the feed sack balanced, bending left to get closer to the keys.

A deeply tanned hand came into her field of vision, and a voice sounded next to her ear.

"Let me get that for you."

She froze halfway down to the ground as Rick popped into view, wearing a hopeful grin.

Chapter Nine

"Hello, Tina."

Rick might as well have said, *Hello, girl parts,* because suddenly, she was on fire. That smile killed her. That and the light in his eyes that sang at her, the way she was sure hers were singing to see him.

She caught a breath then rushed through the next two.

Forbidden, she reminded herself.

Deliciously forbidden, her wolf hummed along.

Rick reached for the sack on her shoulder. "Let me get that."

She swiveled away. "If you could just get the key, please." The horse feed made a handy barrier. Who knows where her hands might go without it to hang on to?

A pair of black eyebrows went up; her heart thumped harder. She and Rick stared at each other for a moment, and a thousand unspoken messages passed back and forth.

Messages like, *I've never forgotten you.*

Like, *I've missed you so much.*

Like, *I've always loved you and always will.*

Their bodies practically hummed with the words. Every part but their lips.

A minute or maybe an hour later, Rick's mouth twitched with a different variation of his smile, and he leaned over for her keys. Then he straightened, dangling them in front of her eyes.

"Trade you for that bag." His baritone was so deep and oaky, it resonated in her bones.

"Thanks, I got it." She ordered her feet to march toward the car.

Rick stepped in her way. "No way am I carrying a key while you carry that bag." He eased it off her shoulder and pushed the key into her hand. "Okay?"

She hated the way he lifted the feed sack like it was nothing, but the flex in his shoulders quickly distracted her. Okay? That was more than okay.

Except it wasn't. She didn't need a man to carry things for her. Especially not this man, whom she could never, ever have.

"Awfully big bag of horse feed for one fish," he murmured as they stepped up to her car.

"What?" She clicked the lock open and popped the trunk, only then remembering the fish in her hand. "No," she laughed. "The kids like feeding the horses their special treat."

His right eyebrow flickered up, and she rushed to clarify. "Not my kids! My nieces and nephew. My brothers' kids. I don't have kids," she blurted and immediately winced.

His lips quirked just a little.

Another awkward pause ensued, which she brought to a disgraceful end with a question she regretted the second it slipped past her lips. "Do you have kids?"

Crap, did she want to know the answer to that? Have the evidence of his sex life stuck right in her face?

"Not yet," Rick said, letting his eyes tango with hers. Hopeful, happily-ever-after eyes that told her just what he meant.

A good thing she wasn't the swooning type. Otherwise she might have keeled over just on the force of those two words. The hopeful lift in his voice, the way he caught his next breath as he waited for her reply.

Her lips moved but couldn't quite find anything to say. What if he was just teasing? What if nine years as a superstar taught him how to make every fan feel like a million bucks?

Tina couldn't tell, because he tilted the feed bag just enough to hide his face, then thumped it into the trunk.

"Well, thanks," she said, slamming the hatchback and breezing to the front door, trying not to notice how closely he followed, or how good he smelled. She fumbled with the key, then turned to face him and immediately gulped. His face was inches away. So close, she could make out the faint scar on his right temple. The kaleidoscope pattern within the honey brown of his eyes. So close, she could kiss him.

Her heart stuttered then hurried on.

"Look, Rick," she started but immediately petered out. Couldn't do anything but look. Remember. Feel.

He stepped a little closer. Boxed her in with his arms.

"Tina." One word. Her name. So why were her knees turning to jelly? Suddenly, she was sixteen again, shy and fluttery-eyed and hopelessly silent.

She ripped her gaze from his, because another second there and she'd be whimpering for something she couldn't have. But her eyes didn't venture past his arms. Corded, muscular forearms. Arms she wanted to wake up in. Arms she had woken up in—far, far too long ago.

Everything in her went pitter-patter, and her inner wolf sat at attention, wagging its tail.

Arms she wanted around her. Now. Forever. All the time.

But he was human and she was wolf. It would never work.

Even if Rick wanted her—even if he had no qualms about her being half wolf—they had no future together. Turning a human into a shifter was a dangerous thing, especially for men. Every shifter knew that. A male wolf could turn a human female into a shifter, but men rarely survived the bite of a female wolf. Something about the chemical change and the way the body fought back. And, the stronger the man, the harder his body would resist the change. Despite the couple of one-in-a-million stories Tina had heard about a female shifter successfully turning a human into a wolf—all of them vague and unconfirmed—she'd heard a dozen grieving stories of things gone wrong. Tragically wrong.

Even if Rick wanted her, even if he embraced the idea of turning half beast—as if that weren't obstacle enough—she could kill him with her bite.

It was no use. Without a mating bite, her shifter lifespan would quickly outstrip Rick's, and she'd be alone. The thirty-plus years she'd already been alone were bad enough; there were another two hundred-plus to come.

If she truly loved Rick, she would let him go. She had to let him go.

"Tina," he whispered, his voice grittier now.

Shifter. Human. Those lines were drawn in the sand.

She flattened her hand against his chest, telling herself it was to push him away and not to count the beats of his heart. The way she'd done their first time together, their second time, and all the imagined times in between. Feeling the steady thump, thump, thump.

She lifted her face, whether to kiss him or tell him to cut it out, she wasn't sure. Either way, it was too late. Much too late. He was leaning in already and instinct had her leaning, too. Stretching up, willing his lips to meet hers.

When they did, a huge sigh coursed through her body. A feeling like the sun coming out after a long, cloudy monsoon. Because his lips were as perfect as they'd ever been, full and soft and savory, and just the right size to slot over hers. His chest was a bed to lay across, his arms thick and firm by her sides.

She kissed him, trying to untangle thoughts of never and forever from the knotted mess they had become. Even though they stood in the parking lot of Arty's Feed & Hardware with traffic rushing past, it felt like she was transported back in time to the leafy shade and peace of Spring Hollow, where they'd first made love. Two giddy teens who thought they'd been exploring each other's bodies when really they were baring their souls. Binding them forever.

Some delayed reaction in her arm made her push against his chest. It barely budged him, but at least it made her point... or whatever point she'd forgotten about midway through that kiss.

"See? You did miss me." He smiled, then went serious. "The way I missed you."

"I can't..." She shook her head, struggling to form words with lips that refused to cooperate on anything but a kiss. "I did miss you. I always do. I always will. But Rick, I can't. I can't have you."

"You can't have happiness?"

48

Her knees wobbled and she dropped her forehead to his chest. What to say to that? *No, I can't. I can't have you.*

"You didn't want to leave Arizona before." His voice rumbled against her chest. "I get that."

Did he? Did he know how much it had hurt her—killed her—to say no and see him go? To see pictures filtering back of him at work—and worse, at play, with supermodel-types appearing on his arm as the camera flashed away? A man like Rick could take his pick from dozens of willing women. Any day, any night.

Of course, he'd always looked a little stiff in those pictures, his smile forced. Not the same shining grin he gave the younger fans. And thankfully, he'd never gotten mixed up in a scandal, never had a steady girlfriend—at least, not one the press caught hold of. Maybe he was just like her, using the occasional lover to take the edge off. Pretending that the loneliness could be remedied by any partner, any night.

"I get that you love it here," he rumbled on.

She did love Arizona. She loved Twin Moon Ranch. But if she could have, she'd have left it all behind for him. Only him.

"But now I'm here. I'm here to stay. So what's stopping us?"

Slowly, gently, he tipped her chin up until she was staring into his eyes. Or rather, blinking frantically to hold back the tears welling up inside.

She could never say it. She could never explain. *Rick, I'm a wolf, and you're human. I could kill you with my bite.*

Then he shook his head and squeezed her into a hug, tucking her head beneath his chin. A good place, she reckoned, to spend the next twenty or so years, hiding from reality.

Eventually, the mountain she was wrapped around lifted and sighed, and two syllables echoed inside. At first she thought it was him, shooting thoughts into her mind the way her packmates could. But it was his voice, resonating through her chest at close range.

"Coffee," he said, pulling back just a bit. "I'm taking you out for coffee."

She blinked. "Coffee?"

"Just coffee," he said, running a hand over her arm. "Just to talk. Not while coming or going, but sitting and taking our time." He leaned in closer, and her heart skipped over the next couple of beats. "Just you and me." Then he shook his head, unsatisfied with the notion of two separate beings, and corrected himself. "Just us."

Chapter Ten

Why did she do that?

Rick looked at Tina, wavering between the *Yes* she seemed so desperate to blurt and the *No* she felt honor bound to throw at him. Why did she always push him away?

Well, he wouldn't push back, but he'd wear her down. Do anything to stretch these minutes with her into hours, at least for today.

"Just coffee," he repeated. Didn't matter that his soul was screaming for more. He had to take it one step at a time. "Please."

"Okay," she whispered at long last.

He almost did a victory dance right there in the parking lot. But he'd never allowed himself that kind of show-off stuff in baseball, and he sure wouldn't pull it now.

"Great," he said, stuffing a million happy-feet dances and fist pumps into that one little word.

She looked up at him with wide, wild eyes, and for a second there, he thought she might come in for another kiss. But then she blinked and pressed something soft and squishy in his hands. "Here, hold Bluey."

He held up the plastic bag full of water and one little fish. It was blue, all right. He looked back at Tina. "Bluey, huh?"

"Greenie needs a new friend."

He cocked his head.

"Don't ask," she sighed and motioned to her car. "I'll drive."

Yeah, that was the Tina he knew. Decisive and confident. Except when it came to him.

He folded himself into the front seat—him and Bluey—
without argument because A, sitting a foot away from her was
a lot better than sitting in a separate vehicle, and B, it did
make sense to take the smaller car into the center of town,
where the streets were full of Old West charm but short on
parking. That was Tina. Sensible.

He closed his eyes as she drove, soaking in her proximity, her
scent. Sensible, but sensual. And sweet, so sweet. Somehow,
her allure had only grown in the years in between.

And just like that, he lapsed into a full-on flashback of the
last night they'd shared together, seven years ago. The way
she melted into his arms. The way her mouth opened when he
slid inside her. The way her legs—

"Is that café fine?" she asked, ripping him out of the memories.

A park bench would have been fine with him. Right here
in the car. Anywhere he got to be with her, sex or no sex.

"Perfect," he said just as a car pulled out from a parking
spot, freeing the space for them. "Our lucky day," he chuckled.
"Fate is on our side."

Tina gaped at him with wide, startled eyes.

What? What had he said?

A car beeped behind them, making Tina's eyes bounce to
the rearview mirror. She muttered something, threw the car
into gear, and parked neatly in the tight spot. Two minutes
later, he was sitting across from her at a corner table in the
shade. Just the two of them.

Okay, plus the blue fish, because the thing would probably
roast to death if they left it in the car.

The coffee came, and he tried to work his way into conversation with her. Tina picked at the tablecloth, intent on the
red-checkered pattern, or the fish, or just about anything but
his face.

"Tell me about Bluey," he tried.

Her smile loosened a little. "Rescue mission for one of my
nieces."

Nieces. Plural? "How many do you have?"

She looked at him for a moment as if to question whether his interest was sincere. And it was. Both his parents had grown up in big, extended families, and that was just about the only regret that ever seeped over from his father to him. That he was an only child, growing up far from dozens of cousins back in Texas.

"Three nieces. Ty has a girl and a boy. Cody has two girls." *And I have none,* her eyes flashed.

His lips moved, and it almost came out. *Me, neither.*

Whenever his dad had come out to visit, his first question was never about Rick's stats or how far away he was from setting a new record, but how far he was from starting a family.

No wife? No kids? When, then? That was his father's measure of a man—if he could cook, and if he was a good family man.

The simple things in life. His dad was a genius.

Rick looked at Tina and his stomach knotted up. So close, yet so far.

He made a quick calculation of how many days of his twenty he had left to win Tina over. And right on cue, an image of Henry Seymour popped to mind. Old Henry would wind up a long list of things to be endured and conquered in twenty days.

The first twenty days of a new job. The first twenty with a new horse. Then Henry would wink and add, *The first twenty days of marriage,* making the missus chide and hide a smile. The love between them was a physical thing, a calico cat that wound around and around their legs, purring.

The same purr that kicked in any time Rick was near Tina.

"Mr. Rivera! Mr. Rivera!"

He dragged his eyes off her and turned them on two kids. "Hi, guys."

"Hi," one boy whispered, slack-jawed now that he was so close.

"Hi," echoed the other, equally tongue-tied.

"Hi," Rick repeated. He didn't mind kids coming up and talking to him, even at a time like this. It was the adults who could be annoying. The ones who liked to show off their knowledge of all the stats of every player in the league. As if numbers said something about the game. As if numbers could bat or pitch, or catch or throw or run.

One kid elbowed the other, who produced a scrap of paper. "Um, could we have your autograph, please?"

"Sure." He scribbled, smiled, and handed it back. Smiled a little more as he watched the kids walk off, grinning like they'd just won the lottery. Turned back to Tina and found her studying him.

"Do you miss it?" she asked, searching his face.

He laughed. "Do I miss people coming up to me all day? I'll be happy when it dies away completely."

She shook her head slowly, sadly. "I mean playing."

He stirred a dash of cream into his coffee and contemplated the swirling pattern it produced. Major League Baseball. Did he miss it?

"At first, I thought I did." Might as well tell her the truth, because going straight from the diamond to Ward D of the trauma clinic was like slamming the brakes on a Lamborghini in the middle of the highway. A trick he hadn't been stupid enough to try the way some of the other guys did. He did take a fancy car for a test-drive once, but he decided a Ford was good enough for him.

In fact, he'd managed to avoid a lot of the stupid things the other young guns did. No bad relationships, no drugs, no arrests. He'd just been standing in the wrong place at the wrong time. That, or destiny had other plans for Ricardo Rivera. Because how else could he explain what happened?

"Maybe the accident was meant to be. It brought me back here, right?" *To you.*

The way she looked at him—looked *into* him, almost— suggested she wanted to believe that, too. Maybe they really were meant to be together, for all that she insisted on denying the crazy pull they had on each other. They were meant to be. They could get together and—

"How did it happen?" she whispered.

He put his coffee cup down. Turned it around. Turned it back. "Didn't you read about it in the paper?"

She turned just pink enough to tell him she'd read plenty. "I never know what to believe in the press."

Smart girl. Because he shuddered to think what was written about him sometimes. About the accident. About his life. About the people who managed to get photographed with him, looking like they actually had some kind of relationship.

"I don't even remember it," he said into the coffee cup. "One minute, I was standing on the sidelines at a high school practice at one of those meet-the-public events. The next, I was in the hospital with a headache the size of Seymour Ranch." That, and an eye bulging half out of its socket, but he'd spare her the gory details. "They told me the kid at bat cracked a real slammer into foul territory. Right as I was leaning over to sign an autograph."

No helmet. No warning. No second chance.

At first, it seemed like the end of the world. But slowly, the crack in his skull healed, the brain swelling went down, and the agonizing headaches became mere migraines. But the nerves around his eye didn't heal, and 80% vision wasn't good enough—not for hitting the kind of balls big-league pitchers threw.

That had taken a while to accept, but yeah, he'd moved on.

Well, was trying to, at least.

Without thinking, he took her hand. Her warmth traveled up his arm and into his chest.

"And then along came Lucy Seymour's addendum to the will and this job. And here I am."

A new beginning, a new chance. His third and final chance at Tina, the way he saw it. A chance at the kind of timeless love his parents had had. Long after his mom passed away, his dad had smiled and called her his princess. The Seymours were the same, weathering the ins and outs of ranch life with a grace fed by their devotion to each other. They were gone now, all of them, buried up on the hill that faced the rising sun, but love was eternal. He could feel it every time he went up there, hear it in the whispers on the wind.

Just like he felt it now between Tina and himself. Love was eternal.

Tina leaned closer, looking so sad, he ached to say more.

"Tina..." he started. How could he put everything into words? That what they'd had together wasn't just puppy love or a couple of horny teens getting lust mixed up with love. That what they had was a one-in-a-million thing. It had taken a while for him to realize that, but he got it now. Yes, there'd been women who made him laugh. Women who made an hour or two speed by. A couple who'd even coaxed a throaty groan out of him. But he'd never, ever met one who made him cry the way Tina did. Never met a woman who made him believe that he could have the kind of love his parents had. Except her. Tina.

He opened his mouth to say it when a cold, hard voice jumped in first.

"My, my. What do we have here?"

Tina jumped; Rick nearly snarled at the sight of Dale Gordon standing by his elbow. His blind side. Again.

"Hello, Dale," Tina said. Her voice was flat, not giving any emotion away. When it had been just the two of them, she wore her emotions on her sleeve. Now she'd slipped on a poker face that revealed nothing, nothing at all.

A woman of class. A princess. *My princess.* The reverent words his father had uttered so often echoed through his mind. They fit Tina perfectly. She'd always had that regal, old-world side to her. But there was a cowgirl in her, too—one who didn't mind getting her hands dirty when the job called for it. Who could work and sweat and grunt with the best of them if need be.

He slammed on the brakes, reeling the image back from where his imagination started hauling it off to like a Viking with his prize.

"Busy day, huh, boss?" Dale snickered.

Rick balled his hands into fists but kept a straight face. If Tina could do it, so could he.

"Apparently, a busy day for you, too," Tina shot right back.

Touché, Rick wanted to crow as Dale's brow furrowed. *Touché.*

"I'd hate to hold you up," she continued, smiling at Dale with an expression that said, *Run along now.* "You must have so much to do."

"Actually, I have plenty of time," Dale said in open challenge.

"I doubt that." Rick stood and stretched to full height, looking down at Dale. Long and hard and unrelenting. The days of Dale running his own show on the ranch while lawyers haggled over wills were over. Rick was the boss now. Not Henry, bless his soul. And certainly not this wash-up of a cowboy named Dale.

I am the boss now. Every cell in his body united to send that message pulsing over to Dale. *I am the boss.*

Dale's eyelid twitched, and his eyes dropped to the floor. His jaw stopped working his wad of chewing tobacco.

Tina grabbed the fish and stood. "See you, Dale. We have to get going."

We. Rick wanted to grab the word and mount it in a frame.

She wove her arm through his elbow and steered him away from the table, leaving Dale behind. And even though Rick could feel Dale shooting daggers at his back, even though he wanted to spin and give the man another withering glare, he didn't. At Tina's touch, the rage building in him eased, giving way to something warmer and mushier. Something much more important than a washed-up old man.

"Hey!" he protested as they walked down the sidewalk. "Don't you know cavemen have to establish rank?"

"Believe me," Tina sighed, "I could write a book about territorial alpha males."

He let her maneuver him to the car and shove the fish in his hands, then nod at the door in a command. "Get in, caveman."

He grinned at her over the roof of the car. "Bossy, much?"

She smiled back, and just like that, they were kids again. Joking, teasing, having fun together.

"I get a lot of practice being bossy, too," she said.

Good, something inside him said. His pulse sky-rocketed again as something primal worked at his insides. The urge to possess this woman and to be possessed.

And the vibes coming off Tina as she drove him back to his truck? They screamed exactly the same thing.

To possess, to be possessed.

Chapter Eleven

Tina shook her head at herself. Having a perfectly innocent—well, mostly innocent—coffee with the man she'd never stopped loving was one thing. Agreeing to meet at his place four days later was another.

Pure business, she reminded herself as she drove down the dirt road connecting Twin Moon with Seymour Ranch. Just one manager helping another out, right?

Her wolf wagged its tail a little too enthusiastically.

Okay, so it wasn't such a great idea. But how could she say no when Rick Rivera, all six foot two, hundred-and-eighty pounds of muscle, had quietly asked for help? A man capable of asking for help was a novelty, given the family she'd grown up in. Her father, her brothers—all powerful, alpha types.

Just like Rick. The man had gone pure, animal alpha with Dale at the café, and Dale had just about shrunk into the woodwork. She couldn't get that out of her mind. If Rick were a wolf, he'd be right up there in the hierarchy with her brother Ty or her father. That raw, male power, that authority. Rick's version, though, was balanced by something softer, more forgiving. Something his mild-mannered father had instilled in him, like the ability to ask for help. The open, easy capacity to love.

She frowned. Rick was so unlike her father in that way. So unlike her grouchy, growly brother Ty, despite the soft side Lana brought out in him. Rick was just so...so...Rick.

In her mind, she replayed his smile and melted all over again. It wasn't a once-a-year phenomenon, like Ty's—okay, once a week, now that Lana was in her brother's life. Nor was it one of Cody's dime-a-dozen smiles, promising everyone he was their best friend—which wasn't exactly a lie, because he practically was, damn him. Rick's smile was warm, genuine, broad. It lit up her world like a goddamn sunrise.

So she'd said yes. *Sure, I'd be happy to help.*

She tapped her fingers on the steering wheel. *Business, pure business.*

Sure, her wolf hummed inside, swiping its tail in long, sultry strokes. *Business.*

She crested the hill leading to Seymour Ranch and drew a deep breath, looking over the familiar features once again. The Seymour homestead, shaded by lazy sycamore, facing the southwest. The big barn on the left and the smaller outbuildings behind it. The paddocks and the bunkhouse on the opposite side. There was something cozy, homey about it, even if it didn't reach out with the same vibrant feel it had when the Seymours were alive. But it had potential. A new paint job would spiff up the house. A couple of new fence posts for the front paddock and it would be ready for that new breed of cattle Henry had been planning to try out. Grain-fed, organic beef; an honest way to work the land. The ruined foundation of the original barn, set back to one side, that would serve perfectly for a greenhouse, where she could—

She caught herself there. This wasn't her home. Not her place to interfere. So what if her heart was leaping half out of her chest at the possibilities?

She coasted down the hill and rolled to a stop at the porch. And just like the first time, when she'd driven up with Ty, Rick emerged from the shade wearing that easy, glowing smile. Moving down the three steps in his graceful, athletic stride.

But this time, her brother wasn't around to chaperone. This time, it was just her and Rick.

Mate. Her wolf nodded inside.

Her soul urged her to jump straight into Rick's arms, while her mind forbade anything but sticking out a stiff hand for a formal shake. Rick solved the stalemate by leaning in for a loose hug and a peck on the cheek. A peck that sent tingles all the way down her spine. Then he turned sideways, draping an arm lightly over her shoulders, and let her lead the way into the house. Giving her space. Letting her choose just how close to walk to him and just how far.

Close, her wolf purred, sidling closer with each step.

Far, her human side barked, trying to summon the willpower to lean away.

She was about to make the sharp turn into Henry Seymour's office, the first room on the right, when Rick tugged her down the hallway, past the grandfather clock.

"Lunch first."

"Lunch?"

She glanced at the walls as they went. Everything was all so familiar, as if she'd been over for Thanksgiving a month before. Everything except the empty feeling of the place these days. The house begged to be filled with the laughter of children, the whispers of lovers, the promise of family.

Their footsteps echoed, amplified by the emptiness until Rick tugged her out onto the back veranda.

"A late lunch," he said as they stepped out of the doorway and into the light.

She caught a breath and held it, rooted to the spot. Held that breath a little longer, because she wasn't quite ready to believe.

The table was covered in one of Lucy Seymour's gorgeous lace tablecloths and dotted with colorful dishes. Feta-stuffed peppers, grilled eggplant. Tamales that could only have been made by hand. Dips, spreads, a salad. A couple of hand-picked desert flowers, popped into a tiny vase. Plus Rick, in a clean white shirt that showed off his bronze skin, pulling out a chair for her.

"Wow," she breathed.

He grinned. "Cook's son, remember?"

She looked at him and nodded slowly. The man must have a bank account that stretched over seven or eight digits, but what did he take pride in? His humble, modest dad. The one with a ready smile, a recipe for every occasion.

"I remember." *I remember him well.*

A bubble of sorrow welled up in her. His father's death had been so brutal, so sudden. So undeserved. But it was all over in such a rush—the investigation, the funeral. Rick had come and gone so quickly, she hadn't even had a chance to see him or say a word.

Words she wanted to say now. *Your father was kind and loving and generous. A good man.*

And God, Rick was exactly the same. Kind. Loving. Genuine, through and through.

Mate. Mine. Her wolf hummed.

She stepped closer, eyes locked on his. Forgetting about business as she let her hand cover his and feel the heat pulsing through it.

Mine. Mate.

Her knees were about to give way, so she slid to the chair and let him push it in. She stared dumbly at the spread as Rick sat kitty-corner from her. And that was another thing. He didn't take Henry's old place at the head; he took a seat around the side. Tina glanced down, realizing he'd seated her in Lucy's usual place. The place of the woman of the house.

Rick sat down and regarded her quietly with eyes that barely hid the hope inside. Her heart thumped in time with the happy strokes of her wolf's tail.

"This. . ." She waved a weak hand toward the spread. "This is gorgeous."

His smile grew; his eyes twinkled. His shoulders stretched just a little wider. "Give it another couple of seasons, and it will really be gorgeous." He nodded toward the garden.

Yes, that part could use some work. It was dry and dusty and overgrown, a shadow of its former glory. But someone had been at work there recently. The left side had just been weeded, the flagstone walkway dividing the left and right halves freshly swept. Somebody cared. Somebody wanted that little part of the past back.

Not just somebody. Rick.

Her fingers itched, eager to dig into the soil right there and then. To turn the flower beds, revive the herbs over in the corner. Make old Mrs. Seymour proud.

"It's gorgeous," she said again.

He smiled wider. "It's a mess."

"Not for long."

His naturally tan skin darkened with a blush as he picked up a fork. "Dig in."

She laughed, then went a little pink at the innuendo her wolf served up at the words.

Yes, dig in, the wolf purred, looking straight at him.

Tina grabbed a napkin and pressed it to her lips before she even took her first bite.

Chapter Twelve

It was the best lunch she'd ever had, bar none. And the best company, too.

Tina dragged her eyes off Rick and anchored them firmly on the bottom of her coffee cup. *Business, pure business.*

Her wolf, though, was pacing and yowling within. *This man is our mate.*

He can't be, she wanted to retort, but she couldn't quite get the words out, not even inside. The best she could come up with is, *He's human, not wolf, and our bite will kill him, not turn him.*

He's strong enough, the wolf urged.

Exactly the problem, she shot back. *He's strong enough to try resisting the change. It will kill him.*

"More coffee?" he asked, lifting Lucy Seymour's antique silver pot. It looked so small, so delicate in his hand.

She wanted to scream at the hills. Holler at destiny. Lodge a formal complaint with fate. Because this was impossible.

He's worth the risk, a whisper snaked out of the hills.

She shook her head. No. She couldn't live with herself if he died.

"No?" Rick shook his head.

Her wolf whimpered inside.

"Maybe we should get started on the books you wanted me to look at."

He looked blank before a flash of disappointment clouded his face. Then the smile crept back. "Sure. That would be great."

"Great," she croaked back.

"Great," he whispered, managing to make even that sound sincere. But that was Rick. Hopeful. Positive. Making the best of things, even if it hurt him inside.

He pulled her chair out, still treating her like a queen, and led the way to the office. Back down the long hallway, past the grandfather clock, ever deeper into the shade of the house. Out of the harsh sunlight and into a private, sheltered world.

She hesitated at the threshold to the office, because the afternoon was not going the way she wanted—needed—it to. She thought she'd be safer from temptation in here. But the urge to give in to the insistent magnetism of the man was stronger than ever.

It could be a secret, the house seemed to hint. *Nobody will know.*

"So," Rick said from over at the big, oak desk, and she had no choice but to step inside. To come around next to him, holding her breath. "These are the books."

She nodded, trying to hear over the roaring in her ears. The office smelled of wood oil and leather, underpinned by Rick's impossibly heady scent. So strong, it was as if fate were fanning his scent toward her. Toward her keen wolf senses, all too eager to suck him in.

This man is ours, her wolf purred. *This man is our mate.*

Rick turned one of the leather-bound ledgers toward her. "I need to check the records, but it's damn near impossible."

Impossible, like resisting that scent.

Books. She slid into Henry's swivel chair, trying to concentrate. Books were familiar territory. She'd be safe as long as she kept her focus there.

Rick angled an open ledger her way. Neat rows of numbers lined up like so many soldiers, ready to march.

"Those are the old ones. Those, I can make out," he said from where he stood behind her. "But the more recent ones— the last of Lucy's, and the books Dale has been keeping—I can barely read." He leaned in to pull another ledger from the pile, and the scent of him rolled toward her like a wave. A wave that called to her to jump in, cool off, revel, and play.

"I don't know if it's me or the books."

She turned, hearing the waver in his voice and found him glaring at the ledgers. A vein throbbed at his temple, right next to the tiny scar. Weakness. Rick had to hate admitting weakness, just like her brothers. He had to hate the need to blink and squeeze his eyes to try to focus on the tiny, scrawling script.

His right arm was braced on the desk at her side, and without thinking, she curled her fingers around his. Maybe the accident wasn't as much in his past as he wanted it to be. Maybe it never would be.

Whether or not the touch helped Rick, she couldn't tell. It sure helped her, though, because the second they made contact, her jumpy nerves calmed down.

Nice, her wolf purred. *Nice.*

She forced her eyes back on the ledger and swept a finger along the page without letting go of his hand. She studied the numbers silently and eventually pulled out another ledger, and another, watching the tidy, round script of the earlier volumes grow lopsided, just as Henry Seymour's body had aged. She turned the page and saw new entries made in Lucy Seymour's lacy handwriting. Then there was a gap, and an entirely new script invaded the pages. Dale Gordon's blocky print. The first few months were legible and in line with the Seymours' conventions—date there, sum there, comment on the right. In the subsequent volume, though, Dale had started leaving out dates, or amounts, and even sticking in question marks. The print leaned more and more heavily, sometimes left, sometimes right, like a drunk winding his way down an alley late at night.

She tilted the page toward the desk lamp.

"It's not you," she assured him. "I can barely make this out."

"But you can read it." For the first time ever, she heard a trace of bitterness in Rick's voice.

"Barely. Now shush." She said it lightly, and his fingers tightened around hers.

His scent surrounded her as he leaned in to read over her shoulder. It was all she could do to keep her mind on the page. She tapped each row before moving on, trying to focus

there. Tap, tap, tap, doing rough sums as she went. Skimming
down the left page then down the right. She leafed to the next
sheet and skimmed again before skidding to a sudden stop and
jumping back a line.

April 17—$85—dynamite for...

She leaned closer, trying to make out the rest. Dynamite
for what?

"What?" Rick asked. His breath tickled her cheek.

She wanted to slide a hand over his cheek and pull him
close.

Concentrate. Just concentrate.

"Dynamite for...for..." The letters were so crooked, she
couldn't make them out. "What would the dynamite be for?"

Rick shifted closer, and everything in her screamed, *Yes!
Yes! Closer!*

"No idea," he murmured.

Destiny, her wolf hummed. *It's destiny.*

Concentrate! She tried, but her heart wasn't in it. Everything blurred together. Hardware bills, invoices from
the vet, and feed receipts crowded on a page she strained
to make sense of. A Post-it note she could barely read.
"Dan...Danielson...Davidson Resources?"

He shrugged.

"Something to do with drawing more water from the
aquifer?"

His face was blank. "There's no plan to pump more water.
I swear there isn't."

The letters on the Post-it were a scrawled bird's nest she
couldn't make sense of, especially with Rick's cheek a hair away
from hers. Warm and just a little stubbly and...wait. His
cheek *was* touching hers.

Her heart skipped faster. Her wolf licked her lips.

She forced herself to lean away but only wound up nuzzling
the arm that caged her in from the other side.

Nuzzling, her wolf murmured. *Good idea.*

It was that or turn and kiss him, because she couldn't *not*
touch him any more. She was powerless against destiny. It was
a magnetic force, sucking her closer and closer. She rubbed her

cheek up toward his shoulder then down, following the bulge of his biceps.

Harder, her wolf demanded. *Rub harder. Mark him as ours.*

She knew she shouldn't. She knew she couldn't. But she did it anyway. She needed it more than she needed to breathe. Needed his scent on her, needed his warmth, his touch.

"Tina," he murmured, nestling closer so his cheek was back on hers.

She'd had dreams like this. Dreams in which they woke up to hours upon languid hours of gentle touches, fluttery kisses, secret smiles. Innocent hours in which she could just be Tina. Not the daughter of the alpha, not the manager of Twin Moon Ranch, not the responsible sister. Just a woman who loved her man. And he could just be Rick. Not the superstar, not the forbidden human. Nothing but the kid next door she'd always, always loved.

She shook her head in a weak no, a last thread of resistance, but all it did was stoke the inner heat.

Mine, her wolf growled and clawed at the last strands of her self-control. *Mate.*

"Rick," she whispered.

He shifted slightly, and then it wasn't just his cheek against hers. It was his lips.

Mine, the human part of her mind echoed. *Mate.*

Chapter Thirteen

A smart man, Rick figured, would have pulled away and cleared his throat when he realized how close he'd gotten. Said sorry and thanks for the help and see you soon. Because you didn't lure a woman into your office for perfectly innocent reasons and then start kissing her just out of the blue.

But it wasn't in him to be that man, not right now. Not with this crazy force field sucking him in. And it wasn't out of the blue, either. That kiss was years in the making. Years of wishing, wanting, dreaming.

That, and Tina's ear begged for a kiss. It *needed* a kiss, the same way she needed to be held and touched and revered. She needed all that as badly as he wanted to provide it. Just like the first time she'd come over with her brother, pretending it was only business, when a man could practically see her soul crying inside.

He blinked and gave his head a little shake, but he still couldn't see straight. The world was getting blurrier, but this time it wasn't his eye. It was Tina, turning his world upside down with her magic touch. While everything was vague and distant, she was perfectly in focus. Each strand of her silky hair, the smooth skin of her cheek. The parallel curves of her ear, the bergamot scent that called to him like nectar to a bee.

Something outside was pulsing, too, like the whole house was cheering him on. Saying, *This woman needs you. Wants you. Loves you.*

Saying, *This was meant to be.*

He felt it deep in his bones, in his heart.

"Tina," he whispered and kissed her ear.

Her eyes were closed. Her head tilted toward his, maybe formulating a secret wish.

Tell me, he wanted to say. *Tell me your wish, and I will dig to the other end of the earth to fulfill it.*

His lips moved right into another kiss, lower this time. Gently, carefully, but another minute of breathing her in and he'd have a hard time stepping on the brakes.

"Tina," he whispered. "Tell me to stop. Tell me now."

Her lips quivered, telling him she wanted this, too. To stop pretending and finally, finally dive into the pleasure on the other side of the invisible line they'd been toeing all afternoon.

"I don't want you to stop," she breathed, sliding her fingers up and down his arm. "I never wanted you to stop."

Her eyes were squeezed tight, like maybe if she didn't look, it would be all right. There it was again, that *something* holding her back.

And just like that, he was tired of that *something*, whatever it was. That *something* had no right coming between them.

He caught her ear between his lips and held it, reveling in her hopeful tremble. Ran his hand through the river of her hair, feeling the silky strands ripple and sway. Leaned deeper, so that his chest touched her shoulder, asking for more. He dipped closer, sliding his lips along her cheek. No way would he let *something* get in the way of what he wanted, not any more.

She let out a tiny whimper, then pivoted and crushed her mouth to his. Kissed hotter and harder than any woman ever had, grabbing his shirt with both hands. Her kisses were all firm, desperate lips and no tongue, because she wasn't teasing or seducing or playing coy.

"Rick," she gasped when she came up for air. "Please don't let me tell you no. Please..." She looked so hungry, so vulnerable with her lips working helplessly in the air. "I want this. I want you."

She rose out of the chair and pulled herself against his chest. He held her tightly, as if he were a split second away from tornado impact and had nothing to hang on to but her. Squeezed her against him and made a vow with every thump of his heart. *I will never, ever let you go.*

He could have held her like that all day, just to make up for lost time, but Tina was a woman possessed. She eased her weight onto the edge of the desk and wound her leg around his waist, shaking with need.

His tongue skimmed the perfect line of her teeth. His lips caught and released hers as a decade of unquenched need blazed high. If other women were water, Tina was champagne, and he could get drunk on her. Already was drunk on her. He nestled closer, pushing his erection along her thigh as she spread her legs wider, guiding him along. Drawing him closer, closer. . . home.

That's just what it felt like. Home. He'd been on the ranch for a week, but this was the first time he had that sense of homecoming. Of throwing his bags down, looking around, and wondering why he ever left. Knowing he never wanted to leave again.

"Tina. . . " he started and immediately forgot what he was going to say.

She tightened her legs around his waist. Let her hands dive under his shirt. Followed the grooves of his ribs, reaching back then pulling forward again. Back and forth, back and forth, until *back* was all the way around to his backbone and *forth* breezed along the line of his abs. Her legs rode ever higher and her hands lower, coming tantalizingly close to the top button of his jeans. Everything in him was bulging for her, not just his cock. His chest puffed out, his breath came faster, the blood pulsed thicker in his veins.

"God, Tina," he said, dipping his mouth to her neck. She tasted just as he remembered her, like cream and honeysuckle laced with the scent of wild bergamot. He nudged closer and she arched into him, hitting every *on* button in his body. Her skin was impossibly soft under his chin, and he had to scrape his jaw along it just for the exhilarating feel of rough against smooth. Man on woman. Hot against hot.

Her arms slid around his ribs and pulled him flush against her chest. Amazing how a woman who was all feminine lines

73

and curves could turn on the muscle when the need arose.

The need for him.

"Tina." He dragged himself away to look her square in the eye. "Be sure."

His heart thumped as she looked up at him with eyes that were wide and dark. A little feral, even.

"I'm sure." She said it so fiercely, it was almost a declaration. A dare. The lonely princess locked in a tower was gone; this was the powerful queen who would absolutely, positively, have her way.

A second later, she was back to princess again, and he was the knight who'd just broken into the tower. She plastered herself against him and whispered again and again, "I missed you so much. So much. . . ."

Funny, he could have said the same thing.

Her fingers got to work on the buttons of his shirt, and his body screamed for more. A wild urge bowled into him—to sweep an arm over the desk, shove everything aside, and lay her back on it. To come down over her, shred the cotton of her top and bury himself inside her, again and again. An urge that could have jumped over to him from Tina, given the way she leaned back, pulling him with her.

His cock was all for it. He'd strip her, taste her, plunge inside. Howl with pleasure and listen to her moan his name. Give himself totally over to the primal need chanting inside. Take. Claim. Possess. He'd—

Whoa. Where the hell did that raging animal come from? He pulled on his inner reins. First of all, he was going to make love to his princess, not fuck her like a wild beast. Second, he was not going to take her here on Henry's desk, much as the idea appealed. He'd been tiptoeing around the ghosts of the Seymours ever since he'd returned, and though something told him they'd approve of the idea of him and Tina together, he was pretty sure they'd be thinking more along the lines of holding hands on the porch swing, not screwing on Henry's desk.

The porch swing scenario, he'd save for later. Much later. Right now, their bodies needed more. A hell of a lot more.

"Tina." He tugged her up.

She blinked as he ran his thumbs along her jawline, keeping close. Making sure this wasn't *no*, but *wait*.

"I want this," he said, so loud it echoed down the hall. "I want you. But here... isn't right."

She turned her hungry gaze from him to the black-and-white portraits hung along the walls. "Where, then?" The urgency in her voice sent a riptide through his bones.

He settled her on her feet, grabbed her hand, and led her out the door. "Follow me."

Chapter Fourteen

Tina went without question, without doubt. She'd had enough denying herself. Enough uncertainty, at least for one day.

That, and her wolf was urging her on like a whole stadium of rabid fans cheering for a home run. With sounds like that filling her ears, she couldn't think of anything but the here and now. The him.

Their footsteps echoed in the hallway, and there it was again, that emptiness, begging to be filled.

Rick didn't take her to the guest bedroom or the living room with its shiny stand-up piano and comfy couch that would have served just fine for what she had in mind. He took her straight out the front door and made a beeline for the barn.

She dug her heels in. "Uh... Rick?"

He turned and it was there in his face: the desire. The urgency. The hunger. "Believe me, I am not taking you to the hayloft." He grinned, and a little bit of the devil crept into his face. "Or the back seat of a car."

And zing—another shot of lust bolted through her, because they had done it in the back seat of a car when they were teens. Just the memory of it was better than any of the sex she'd had with any other man in all the intervening years. She and Rick had also done it in the hayloft, and best of all, that time out in Spring Hollow, under the stars. He had a way of picking offbeat places to make love to her in, she had to give him that. But the barn?

He tugged her hand. "You'll see."

She wanted to see. See and touch and taste and feel him moving inside her.

His fingers tightened again, and they were off. Around the corner of the barn, up a set of exterior stairs, and in through a door at attic level. Through another door and—

She caught her breath as Rick pushed it open, revealing a gleaming white-walled apartment built under the eaves. An open-plan, studio apartment where earth-toned Mexican tiles and diamond-patterned Navajo rugs led to a huge bed with yellow sheets. The pitched roof of the barn peaked high in the middle and sloped down on the sides, framing a heart-stopping view of the desert between the A-shape of its rough-hewn beams.

"What. . . " She trailed off.

"The Seymours had the idea to make a little money on the side with a vacation place. You know, weekend ranch getaways for city types? But it never really took off."

She couldn't imagine why. Though, right now, she didn't much care.

"It didn't feel right to move in to the house, so. . . " He trailed off, looking around the room.

She followed his gaze. He'd personalized the space with a picture of his parents smiling over a tiny bundle that must have been baby Rick, once upon a time. That and a picture of him and his ever-smiling Dad overlooking the paddocks. Not a single baseball shot, not a framed uniform in sight.

She pulled him into another hard kiss. This man was the real thing. Pro baseball hadn't taken the humble out of the farm boy. But man, was she glad he hadn't moved back in to the bunkhouse his family used to share with Dale's. This was much, much better.

He wrapped his arms around her, held her close, and nosed her ear, sending tingles up and down her spine.

Closer, her wolf hummed. *Need him closer.*

Damn beast. *How close can this man come?*

Inside, the wolf yowled. *Deep, deep inside.*

And there she went again, her inner temperature soaring off the charts.

"You don't have a three-date rule, do you?" he chuckled, sliding a hand inside her shirt.

She laughed. A wolf with a three-date rule? "No."

"Good." He smiled, and she just about melted.

"Don't stop, Rick." She dipped her thumbs inside the front of his jeans, aching to dig deeper. "I want you to keep going."

He raised one perfect eyebrow. Dark and dashing, that's what he was, like a Spanish Don. A conquistador, all cleaned up and ready to live a quieter life. "Keep going until...?"

The tease. Well, two could play at that game.

"Until I beg," she said, popping the button of his Levi's.

"For what?" he murmured. His eyes were hooded, his chin set hard.

"For more. And more. And more." She slid the zipper down slowly, stopping to punctuate every word. "I want you to touch me." She slid her hands around his waist and snuck them in the back. "Taste me. Fill me."

His eyes shone, his fingers flexed over her waist. The tease was gone, replaced by a very hungry cowboy. "Tina..."

She stepped backward toward the bed. "Just do it, cowboy."

"It?"

"Me. Do me."

He lowered her to the bed with a smile that could have stopped traffic in downtown Phoenix. Make that one of those freeways in LA that Californians spent half their lives commuting along. The minute she sank into the mattress, he went back to work on her neck. Kissing. Nipping. Driving her higher and higher.

She turned her ear to the bedding to give him better access to the left side of her neck, and just like a true wolf, he went right for the nook under her chin where her pulse beat, hard and thick. As if something instinctual drew him there.

Bite me. Take me. Make me yours, her soul sang.

He sucked in the hollow, then nipped the skin, and her whole body jerked in delight. Then he was back at her mouth with a kiss that was five levels hotter and harder than before, giving his passion free rein.

She found the hem of his shirt and worked it up his body, inch by luscious inch, enjoying the ride. Her fingers had to spread wider and wider as they slid upward, following the vee of his torso up and up and up. Pausing at his nipples, rubbing them with her thumbs. Tweaking the tiny nubs, tracing the flat expanse of his chest.

He sucked in a sharp breath and closed his eyes as she let her fingers wander over the fine topography of his chest. The wide fields of his pecs, the shallow valley in between. The layers of muscle stacked on each other like so many intersecting planes.

God, the boy next door had done a lot of growing since the last time they'd met.

"Nice," she breathed. "Very nice. You been doing some cattle-lifting on the side?"

He flashed another panty-melting smile before ducking the rest of the way out of his shirt. "Just the usual workout. Keeps me sane."

Sane. Right. He was driving her out of her mind.

She tossed the shirt aside. Their fingers tangoed briefly until she slid free to trace the taut curve of his rear. More muscle. More power. His erection was hard against her stomach, begging for release.

"Too many clothes," she murmured, tugging at his jeans.

"Way too many," he agreed, working the top button of her blouse.

He didn't get far, though, before she slid a hand inside his jeans and made his whole body go stiff.

Stiffer, her wolf corrected. *Very nicely stiff.*

Gingerly, her fingers explored their prize, wiggling the jeans away. Rick went stone-still except for the ripple that went through his back.

"Well, well, what do we have here?" she teased.

His next breath was a heavy huff, his voice a groan. "Don't tell me I have to explain."

She pulled his boxers over the hard ridge then pushed them away and kicked them over the side of the bed. "I think I can figure this out."

He laughed, but it was a choked, throaty sound. "I'm sure you can."

"Remember our first time?" She ran both hands over his hard length.

He chuckled, and somehow, she'd never felt closer to him than right then. "Like I'd ever forget."

She smiled, because she really had needed to figure it out, their very first time. A couple of breathless teens sneaking off, eager to go all the way. She'd had to figure out how tightly to hold him, how fast to slide. When to give and when to take.

This time around, she was guided by experience and abundant tactile clues. His thick, pulsing shaft. The moisture building at the cleft in the velvety tip. She laced her fingers together and cupped him that way, sliding until she reached the thatch of dark curls signaling the end of the ride, then gliding back up. Up, up, up over the length of him, until she was teasing the tip again, tugging the foreskin. He lay suspended over her with his biceps bulging, his eyes closed like a man listening to a faraway tune. Then his eyes popped open, showing sheer, primal need.

"Too many clothes," he mumbled, eyeing her like a pirate who'd been away from shore for far too long.

He kissed her then pulled away, kneeling between her legs. His eyes grazed over her, spread out on the bed before him.

"Too many clothes," he repeated in a voice gone low and gritty.

It was a quiet order, because he didn't move. His eyes focused on the top button of her shirt.

Too many clothes.

Something in her purred. A man who knew what he wanted. A man with a soft touch but firm demands who knew just how to make her want to give, give, and give.

She slid her hands along her body, pretending they were his until she found the top button and watched his eyes flash with commands.

That one, his eyes said.

She slid the button through the slot and waited, barely breathing.

The next one.

She popped it open, revealing the top edge of her bra.

His eyes went darker. *Next.*

She almost wished she'd worn that calico dress she had, the one with a tight row of buttons. Dozens of them, side by side, just to prolong this pleasure.

One more.

An alpha, through and through. Too bad he wasn't a wolf. But right now, not even that mattered. Just the unbearable hunger that only this man could quench. She popped the button then wiggled down the mattress, just far enough along to reach his cock with her free hand.

Rick's chest heaved in a long, deep breath. His cock twitched in her fingers as she stroked.

Her wolf howled. *Mine! Mate!*

The rest of the buttons. Faster, his eyes urged.

Faster turned out to be easy, because she was burning up inside. The slick weight of him in her hand, the hunger in his eyes... *Faster* was a damn good idea.

She popped the bottom button, spread the flaps of her shirt wide along with the cups of her front-hook bra, and slid both hands to his cock, waiting.

"Your turn," she whispered in a husky voice.

He splayed two wide, brown hands on her waist. "My turn."

Chapter Fifteen

Tina held her breath, watching Rick watch her. Deciding. Imagining. Plotting. Or so she hoped, because she was ready to be shaken, taken, driven howling mad.

"Rick..." She was about to hurry him up, but he swept both hands up at exactly that moment, cupped her breasts, and dove in.

He consumed her. Held her, nipped her, worked her over until she couldn't see straight. She arched higher and higher against him, desperate for more of his mouth on her breast, more of those teeth scraping her soft skin, more of his tongue laving her nipple. He sucked, bringing her right to the border between pleasure and pain before releasing the nipple and switching over to the other side.

Her wolf howled inside, and some of the sound slipped out until she was singing to the ceiling. Moaning all kinds of incomprehensible things. The only word that sounded like anything was his name.

"Rick..." She mumbled it again and again.

When he came up for a breath, his eyes were flashing and dark.

"More," she moaned, shuddering under his touch.

He cupped her left breast, caught her nipple, and circled it with his tongue. His right hand swept down her body and under the hem of her jeans.

"Tell me what you want," he whispered, tapping a finger close, so close.

Her hips practically jumped off the mattress. "I want you."

Just when she'd nearly maneuvered herself closer to his finger, he slid back.

"Tell me."

"I want you."

"Where?"

Where? She wanted him everywhere. "Tell me you don't need step-by-step instructions."

He grinned. "What if I did?"

Right. Like he would. Even their first time, way back when, he'd honed right in.

"I think I might scream. And not the good kind of scream," she added, just to get him back.

His nostrils flared like a bull about to charge. He liked that idea, all right.

She gave a weak kick. "Too many clothes, remember?"

"I can take care of that."

He backed down and pulled her jeans off. Her panties, too. Shucked them both together and tossed them out of reach so she wouldn't get any bad ideas about retrieving them any time soon.

She thought he'd climb back onto her and tease a little more, but he stayed there at the edge of the mattress, gazing at her with those flashing Zorro eyes. His eyes widened when her chest rose on a breath, and his cock stood high and proud.

He muttered to himself and slid both hands up her legs. Up, up, up, with his thumbs on her inner thighs, climbing higher and higher. He might as well have been sliding a temperature gauge, because her body heated as he moved. Jumped into open flames when his thumbs met her sex.

"Rick," she moaned.

"I want to see you," he murmured, sliding his hands down to her knees and pushing them apart. And then he slid his hands up again, slowly.

"Oh, God. Rick." He was killing her, going that slowly, but it felt so good.

Up, up. He rolled upward, setting every nerve clanging on the way. And when he touched her folds. . .

"Rick!" she cried as he spread her wide.

He didn't say anything. Just watched her squirm and dance under his touch. He slid his thumbs this way and that, experimenting. Perhaps taking mental notes on how Tina Hawthorne liked it most: where, how, at what angle, and how hard.

"Is that good?"

"Rick..." she moaned, because all of it was good. Too good.

One blunt end of his thumb teased at her entrance. When it slid in, she just about popped off the mattress. Her head flopped around on twisted sheets as she murmured incomprehensibly.

His fingers mined deep, then stretched apart.

"Yes..." she mumbled.

Somehow, she held on while he circled, tickled, and scissored inside. She soared higher and higher until all she saw was the white of the clouds.

"I need you, Rick," she groaned. "Come with me."

One thick finger pushed deeper.

"Please. Rick. Come," she begged.

He folded over her and groaned in her ear. "Need a condom."

She could have screamed. Wolves didn't need condoms. But how could she explain? *Rick, I know I'm behaving like a bitch in heat, but I promise I'm not actually in heat. And not only that, but wolves are immune to human diseases.*

"No. No condom." She raked at his back, trying not to scratch in her desperation. "I promise. I'm good. We're good."

He studied her for a moment, indecision tearing at his face. "Tina..."

"I swear." She tugged at his shoulders. "Please..."

His lip quivered, and then he gave in. He crawled higher to kiss her, and though it started as a gentle touch, it ended up a tornado. She wiggled under him, lining up under his hips, wrapping her legs around his waist.

"Rick..."

He slid in with one blinding push.

"Yes!" she cried, urging him deeper.

He bottomed out but kept up the pressure, pushing hard. She could feel the stretch, the heat, the sheer power inside.

"So good," she mumbled, telling herself it was real. Not a dream. Real. "So good."

The tornado jumped into his eyes, and she wondered what her own eyes were showing. Were they swirling like this whirlpool she felt swept up in? Glazed over? Sparkling with lust?

Rick squeezed his lips tight and pulled back, then thrust back in.

"Jesus, Tina..."

"More," she moaned, pulling him in.

He thrust in and out, in and out. It took her a minute to match his rhythm—a long, hot minute that was a high in and of itself. Then they moved in perfect sync, her hips bucking up as his drove down, her hands squeezing, her inner muscles clamping down harder and harder. So hard even Rick started to groan.

If she had him in her hand, she'd play him like a piano, striking one note after another as she moved down the keys. Her hands were busy on his sculpted ass and his cock was buried deep, deep inside, so she mimicked the motion with her inner muscles, rippling over him from top to bottom.

He groaned long and hard against her neck. "Again." His voice was raspy and low. "Do that again."

She pumped again, and he groaned. Then he set off on another series of insistent thrusts, working her up the mattress in tiny increments until the rhythm shattered into a dozen wild plunges. They both hung on, neither one of them in control. All instinct, all nature, all heat, until they tipped over the edge and went flying. Rick shuddered and went hard all over, his eyes squeezed shut. Tina convulsed, soaring away on a high like none she'd ever imagined. When she finally wafted back to earth, they were both panting and limp in the sheets, flush with satisfaction and wonder. Her fingers were clutching the sheets, and it took a conscious effort to let go. She never wanted to let go, not of any part of this.

She counted the beats of his heart, the grooves of his ribs, the individual hairs curling around his ears. Counted and held on and did her best to record it for all time, just in case.

When Rick pushed back on his elbows, she nearly protested, but stopped when he cupped her face with both hands and looked into her eyes, drinking her in.

"Tina..." he started.

Part of her wanted to hear the words she saw poised on the tip of his tongue. *I love you. Stay with me. Be mine and let me be yours.*

The very words he'd spoken to her a long time ago, begging her to come away with him.

But hearing them would shatter her, because she couldn't say yes. So she pulled him back into a kiss. Right now was about right now. And later... Well...

She sighed and hid her face against his neck.

Chapter Sixteen

Tina cracked an eyelid open, then immediately closed it again. That light slanting past the panoramic windows wasn't coming from the east. It couldn't be. Somehow, she'd gotten turned around. That had to be west, and it was dusk, not dawn, right?

She shut her eyes tightly. Dusk. It had to be. It might be conceivable that her quick afternoon business meeting had turned into a whole afternoon of unbridled passion, but there was no way—*no way*—she'd ever allow herself to indulge in an entire night of sex. Not even with Rick.

Could she?

But a rooster was crowing, the cattle lowing, and the scent wafting through the open windows was that of the chuparosa with its sweet scarlet flowers. The barn owl had long since stopped hooting, and the air was cool. Too cool for evening.

Her eyes popped open and took in the pinkish-yellow light of dawn.

Oh, God. Dawn?

Her inner wolf yawned and rolled over. *Too early to get up. Much too early.*

It wasn't too early. It was late. Much too late! She couldn't believe what her inner beast had made her do.

Right, like it was me howling at the ceiling last night. Her wolf grinned. *Like it was me running my fingers down our mate's chest, begging for more. Like it was me—*

She jammed her hands over her ears to squelch the inner dialogue. Enough, enough. God, what had she done?

You done good, the beast sighed dreamily. *The best night we've had in years. Maybe forever. Just us with our mate.*

Rick's arm was still snug around her waist. His chest warmed her back, and she sighed in spite of herself.

Our mate, the wolf repeated, just to reinforce its point.

Images of the previous night flashed through her mind, some quick, others in super slow motion. Like Rick, lying over her, his jaw clenched as he thundered into another incredible high. Rick, flat on his back, looking up with a glazed expression that said there was no greater privilege than being ridden by her. Rick, snuggled face-to-face with her, smiling that little-boy-all-grown-up smile.

She drifted away on that smile, entangled in intimate memories that pushed away the fear and doubt. The more she held on to them, the more the images boiled down to simple things. A warm bed. A soft touch. A good man. One with just the right amount of hard in just the right places.

She blinked back into real time, and there he was, smiling at her again.

"Good morning." His voice rumbled through the crisp morning air.

Good morning, my love, her wolf prompted.

What a morning it would be if she truly got to say that.

"Good morning," she whispered back.

And suddenly, she was stuck, because she'd never ever woken up with a man. With wolves, there were no mornings-after. Whether in human or canine form, it was all the same: they screwed hot and hard then got on with life. No awkward wake-ups, no empty promises, no regrets. The few human lovers she'd had, she tumbled away from before they got too attached, because she could never, ever allow a human too close.

And yet here she was, smiling at Rick in spite of herself. He was impossible, just impossible to resist.

Destiny, her wolf grinned.

Like that was a good thing. Like destiny cared that the only way forward for their love led to tragedy.

"Beautiful," he murmured, reaching out to smooth her hair back. He ran a finger over her right eyebrow then leaned in with a kiss. A kiss so good, so true, that she forgot about destiny and tragedy for another blissful minute or two.

Or twenty, or thirty, because the kiss got away from her. And just like that, she was wrapped around him again, making crazy little whimpering sounds while their bodies worked their magic one more time.

I love you.

It was in his eyes and on the tip of her tongue when they lay clasped together afterward, and she might just have let it slip if the phone hadn't rung.

Let the damn thing ring, her wolf growled.

"Just leave it," Rick whispered a little more diplomatically.

But the phone rang and rang, and damn it, rang a little more.

She rolled off the bed, fished through the clothes strewn around the studio apartment like confetti, and pulled it out of her jeans pocket.

"Hello?"

Rick rolled off the bed behind her and padded over to the coffee machine in the apartment's tiny kitchenette.

"Morning, Grumpy," her brother's cheery voice replied.

"Cody?"

"No, it's Ty," he joked, lowering his voice to a grumble. "Can't you tell?"

"Very funny, Cody. What do you want?"

"Well, seeing as you seem to have had a late night..." He let the words hang in the air for ten slow seconds before clearing his throat loudly and finally continuing. "And since I couldn't find you this morning as you seem to have gone out really, really early... Like predawn early, or maybe even forgot to come home..." His voice dripped with innuendo. Damn her little brother!

She stirred the air with her hand and used the nickname no one had spoken in years. "Get to the point, little man." If her six-foot brother had a point other than to tease her, that is.

"Right. Well, I was going to pick up Carly today, but there's been a report of trouble out of the east side—"

Her heart thumped harder. Hellhound? "You mean, the...the..." She couldn't exactly say it, not with Rick right there.

"Maybe. Look, I have to check it out with Kyle, so I need you to pick up Carly. Her flight comes in at nine."

Her eyes flew to the clock. She'd just make it if she rushed.

"Of course, if you're too busy," Cody said, slipping back into surfer dude tone, "I can tell Ty and ask him to pick—"

"No!" she yelped into the phone. It had taken years to get her father and older brother to accept that she was all grown up, and even so, they still used the stare of death on any male suspected of fooling around with her. Rick, they'd kill on the spot. "Cody, if you so much as—"

He laughed. "Just kidding. Unfortunately." He gave a theatrical sigh. "I owe you forever for helping me win my mate, so I'll have to let you off the hook. This time." She could see the wink hidden in his words. "But it would be a big help if you could get Carly."

"I will. But you owe me."

"I do owe you." His voice was serious for a change.

She clicked off, sighed, and looked up to find Rick— gloriously naked Rick—handing her a steaming mug of coffee.

She blinked. Coffee? When was the last time anyone had made coffee for her?

Apart from Aunt Jean on the occasional quiet afternoon, nobody. Ever.

"*Café con leche.*" He smiled and pulled her back to bed, where he lay down, propped on one elbow. "Just like my dad used to make."

She took a sip, placed the mug on the side table, and curled up beside him like a cat, perfectly at home. Just like in her dreams, it was her and the love of her life, waking up together, starting a day together. The ultimate fantasy, because they were both naked, too. Her mind threatened to run away on that one, but she reeled herself back in. She couldn't allow herself any more fantasies or any more mornings. This had to be it.

"I have to go," she mumbled, although her body refused to budge.

He rubbed a thumb across his chest in that absent gesture she loved so much. "Yeah?"

"I have to pick up my sister at the airport."

His eyebrows shot up. "You have a sister?"

"Carly. She lives in California with her mom." She cursed inside, because her voice was suddenly wistful and weak, like it always was when she wondered how different life would be if she'd had a mother to live with. Just to talk to, even, from time to time.

Rick studied the swirl of milk in his coffee, lost in his own thoughts. Was it worse to be left behind by a mother who'd run out, she wondered, or to lose a loving mother to cancer far too young, as Rick had?

When he finally took a sip, it ended up being a heavy gulp, and he winced a little. Her, too. Then he flashed a tight, bittersweet smile. Like he knew just what she was thinking. Maybe even wondering the same thing.

She took his hand and held it, and the warmth traveled up her arm, making her chest swell just a little bit. A little more when he pulled her knuckles to his lips and kissed them without saying anything.

Over in the main house, the grandfather clock bonged. Eight o'clock.

"I have to go," she whispered.

He smiled that tight, bittersweet smile and kissed her knuckles one more time.

"No breakfast?"

She shook her head slowly. Sadly. No breakfast. No mornings. No more.

Chapter Seventeen

"See you soon?" Rick forced his voice to be steady.

Tina's gaze fluttered to the ground, to the wilted flower beds, to the road. Anywhere but to him.

"See you soon," she whispered, and then she was gone.

Rick stood on the Seymours' porch, watching the dust cloud of her Corolla rise to the pale autumn sky for a long time after she drove out of sight. He stared into the distance as the dust slowly settled again.

He kicked at the dirt and sighed.

Tina. He'd stayed up a long time after she fell asleep, just looking at her, and woke up early to do the same thing. He could run a finger along her back, her eyebrow, her hip again and again and never get tired of it. He could get old happily and even go blind in the other eye, as long as he could still feel her, touch her, sense her at his side.

He'd have thought they'd more than made up for lost time with the number of orgasms they'd both hit, but his fingers still flexed in empty air, wishing for her back. Because there was the high that came with sex, and there was the peace of coming home. He raised his nose to the desert air, sniffed like a dog, then chuckled to himself. Tina definitely brought out the animal in him.

See you soon. How soon?

His fingers tapped together as he walked, calculating how many of his twenty days he had left.

He turned on his heel and headed inside the Seymour homestead. Stopped in the doorway before going in, letting his eyes adjust to the dim light until he could make out the hands of the grandfather clock and the lines on the black-and-white artwork on the wall. A Picasso print—the one Mrs. Seymour told him about when he was a kid. The wobbly stick figure was Don Quixote, who chased after windmills and did all kinds of other crazy things.

Chasing after windmills, old Henry would chime in. *Like us running this ranch.*

They'd laugh at that, the Seymours, and smile at each other and carry on. They never gave up, not in tough years, not through the droughts, not when outsiders came along with offers that were too good to be true. And he'd do the same. The ranch had a lot of potential. He knew he could get it back on its feet—without resorting to crazy plans like selling water rights or any such nonsense. Why would Tina's brother think he'd ever do such a thing?

The wind breezed down the empty hallway, prompting a sigh. The only souls left on the ranch were him, old Dale in the bunkhouse, and a couple of ranch hands who came and went. Yesterday, with Tina here, the whole place seemed to have perked up, but today, it was as tired and worn and empty as it had been before.

He turned the corner for the office and came to an abrupt halt.

The door was open, and Dale sat reclined in the chair with his dirty boots propped on Henry Seymour's oak desk.

"Dale," Rick gritted out. The soaring updraft that he'd been gliding on suddenly petered out and dropped him in a dusty heap.

Dale barely looked up. Barely acknowledged him there. Lazily turned a page of a ledger before stabbing his cigarette out on a saucer over by the lamp. The delicate saucer that was part of Lucy Seymour's china set, painted with a pheasant and flowers and grass. There was nothing delicate about the stale smell of tobacco, though, or the stale smell of the ranch foreman.

Rick counted slowly to ten.

"Have a nice sleep-in, boss?" Dale said, tossing him one of those crocodile smiles.

The man might as well have said, *Blowing off work again?*

Rick scowled. "Get your feet off Henry's desk."

Dale shifted his feet into a more comfortable position. "Your desk, you mean. Boss." He added the final word a split second after the rest. Trying to push Rick's buttons, as usual, though it would never work.

"Henry's desk," Rick growled back.

"Not sayin' a man doesn't deserve a little lie-in, not with company like that." Dale faked nonchalance, tilting his head in the direction Tina had gone.

That button worked. Rick thumped both hands on the desk and all but roared in Dale's face. "Get. Out. Of. This. House."

That got Dale moving. Faster than he'd ever seen the man move, as a matter of fact. Rick kept his hands on the desk lest they throttle Dale as he scrambled past. One more comment, one more hint, and he'd kill the man with his bare hands.

He stood there a long time afterward, fighting to settle his nerves. Yeah, Tina definitely had a way of bringing out the animal in a man.

Chapter Eighteen

"Carly!" Tina waved, spotting her sister at last. She'd pushed the speed limit and run more than her share of yellow lights to get to the airport in time, but she'd made it.

"Tina!" Carly strode over from the security checkpoint.

A dozen heads turned, as they did wherever Carly went. Her long blond hair flowed like she'd just stepped out of a shampoo commercial. Mile-long legs stuck out in the ample space between her ultrashort cutoff jeans and ultrahigh cowgirl boots, showing a golden tan. The pink tank top she wore hugged her trim figure so tightly, Tina could make out the ring Carly wore in her pierced navel.

Carly shook off three would-be suitors like flies just in the course of covering those thirty feet. Walked right past them, exuding that I-couldn't-care-less-what-you-think attitude she'd been born with. She strode across the tired carpet of the airport and stepped casually into Tina's hug.

"Hey, baby sis," Tina murmured. Even with Carly being Carly, it was good to see her again.

"Hi, old lady," Carly shot back. She patted Tina on the back, then froze. Sniffed. Pulled back to study Tina's face.

Oh, shit. Tina cringed. *Here it comes.*

"Yum," Carly announced, loud enough for half the crowd to hear. She leaned in for another sniff. "He smells good."

Shit, shit, double shit. Her sister's keen shifter nose had zoned right in on Rick's scent. God, what had she been thinking last night, rubbing up and down Rick like that?

We were thinking mate. *Remember?* her wolf chimed in.

Tina grabbed her sister's arm and hauled her down the concourse. "Shh!"

"It's not like these people know you!" Carly laughed, tossing her golden hair.

Four different men tripped over their own feet just watching her, and even the priest standing beside a newsstand looked ready to break his vows. *Carly-traffic*, as Cody called it. The woman created gridlock everywhere she went.

Tina dragged her along by the elbow as two men bumped into each other. "Next time, I'll let Cody pick you up."

"Next time, I ride my Harley. I hate flying." Carly sniffed.

Every inner alarm in Tina clanged as she stopped in her tracks. "Wait a minute." She took Carly by both shoulders. "You didn't crash another motorcycle, did you?"

Carly rolled her eyes. "No, *Mom*. I'm just here for three days this time, so I decided to fly."

Tina studied every inch of her sister's lithe frame for fresh scars. Shifters healed quickly, but if you looked hard enough... The faint scratches across one shoulder were from the time Carly totaled her last bike in an accident that would have killed any human. The jagged line across her right forearm from one of her rock climbing falls was still there, too.

"Good." Tina finally nodded. "Flying is safer." Anything where Carly wasn't at the controls was safer.

Her sister flashed a wicked smile as her eyes took on that wild look. "Maybe next time I will ride the bike. Really let that puppy fly..."

"Don't even joke about it," Tina barked, towing her down the hallway again.

Her heart was thumping now, because yes, as older sister and sole Hawthorne female at the ranch, her motherly instincts were always hard at work. And they worked double time whenever her daredevil sister was around.

Daredevil? Death wish is more like it, the ranch women used to mutter. Tina had always shushed them, because you never knew. Carly might try living up to those words just to prove that she could.

"Ha!" Carly pointed at the luggage belt. "Mine's the first one out!"

That was the thing about Carly; she had a lucky streak a mile wide. A good thing, too.

"Buckle up," Tina reminded her the minute they slid into the car.

"Sure thing." Carly buckled it behind her back so the alarm would stop dinging. She leaned back and rested her feet on the dashboard.

"What if we get rear-ended? What if an eighteen-wheeler wipes us out?"

Carly yawned. "We're shifters. We'll heal."

"One of these days..." Tina was afraid to say the rest. That shifters were still mortal, and a bad enough accident on an unlucky day...

Carly cranked up the air conditioning and changed the subject. "How do people live in this climate? I swear it's a hundred and twenty."

"A hundred and seventeen," Tina murmured, merging onto the highway. "Here in Phoenix. But up at the ranch—"

Carly took over from there. "At the ranch, it's a perfect eighty-nine. At the ranch, everything is perfect. You sound like Dad."

Tina scrunched her lips together, but Carly just laughed. "Now you even look like Dad."

Which was easy for her to say, because Carly, like Cody, was lucky enough to take after her mother: free-spirited, gorgeous, outgoing. Tina and Ty, on the other hand, had been cursed with their father's genes. Striking dark looks were one thing, but she could have done without that leaden mantle of duty, the excruciating attention to detail that made her nearly as hard to please as her father.

"So, is old man Atsa still going on about this hellhound?" Carly asked.

Tina tsked. "It's a legitimate concern, Carly."

"Is it? Anything new?"

She had Tina there. A week had gone by since Atsa's warning, and they had no concrete evidence that the Navajo shaman hadn't raised another false alarm. The constant vigilance was wearing everyone down, and to be honest, they'd all eased off a bit. Patrols still scoured the countryside and the neighboring packs communicated regularly, but none had found any sign of a demon.

"Cody called this morning and said he was checking on the latest report, but he didn't sound too convinced."

"Wait, Cody *called* you to say this?" Carly eyed her closely, then cracked into a grin. "Oh, I get it. You were with Cowboy Delicious, so you weren't at home." Her face lit up with mischief. "So, okay, tell me about him. I want details." Carly rubbed her hands together. "Gory, orgasmic details."

Tina rolled down the window for some fresh air. Maybe trying to clear a little of Rick's lingering scent, too. A futile attempt, because she'd rubbed him hard enough to make his skin shine, but it was worth a try. "Don't tell anyone, okay?"

"Why not?" It was a challenge, not a question. Almost a dare.

"Carly," she ground out. "Do. Not. Tell. Anyone."

"Why not? You have a right to screw any cowboy you want, Tina. To hell with what Dad says."

Easy for her sister to say. Tina kept her eyes steadfastly on the highway ahead. It was easy for Carly to be Carly. Independent. Reckless. Unafraid. Carly hadn't grown up as the oldest daughter of the ruling alpha. She didn't manage a ranch and concern herself with things like her reputation, because she didn't carry a mile-high stack of expectations or have a hundred invisible judges studying every move she made, every day.

"He sure smells good." Carly leaned in closer, sniffing.

Tina leaned away and rolled the window open a bit more.

"Man, that scent is strong. Did you shag him all morning and most of the night?"

She must have blushed, because Carly broke out in a huge grin and smacked her on the shoulder.

"You did shag him all morning and most of the night! Way to go, girl!"

"It's not like that," Tina tried.

"No? Then what was it like?"

Like magic. Like heaven. Like the best parts of every sweet dream rolled into one night.

Tina squeezed her lips together and looked straight ahead. Carly would never understand. Thank goodness Carly hadn't spent enough time in Arizona to remember Rick's scent, because the only thing worse than her sister knowing *about* Rick was her sister realizing *who* Rick was. She could hear the screech now.

Rick Rivera, the star hitter? You fucked Rick Rivera?

If she hadn't been driving, she would have buried her face in both hands.

Carly chuckled. "You're in love, aren't you?"

Every muscle in Tina's body tensed. "What do you know about love?"

"I've fallen in love!"

Tina arched an eyebrow at her sister.

"I have!" Carly waited a beat, then waved vaguely. "So, okay, I fell back out..."

"Then it wasn't love."

Carly snorted. "What is love anyway? I mean, true love."

Tina opened her mouth. Closed it. Opened it again. "True love is...is..." She was a little short on words, but images flooded her mind. Rick, pulling out the chair for her at lunch. Rick, his jaw tight as he said he understood about her not wanting to leave Arizona with him. Rick, gazing into her eyes like they were a wishing well and he was down to his last penny.

Carly took in her silence with a weighty nod. "Wow. You really are in love."

Tina wanted to cry, to kick, to scream. She'd been in love with Rick all her life, but no one ever asked. Ever suspected. Ever cared. Not about Good Old Tina.

"You're actually serious about this guy?"

"How can I not be serious? He's my destined mate." She blurted it out before thinking, then slapped a hand over her mouth.

Carly was too busy shaking her head to notice, thank God. "There is no such thing as a destined mate. You of all people should know that."

"There is," Tina said fiercely. "There is!"

"Is not," Carly retorted. "Just regular old love, just like any human."

Tina's wolf started growling inside.

Carly galloped off on one of her tirades. "Look, am I glad the right woman came along and knocked some sense into Ty's head? Of course I am. Am I glad Heather got Cody to grow up? Hallelujah, I say! Good for her. But it's not destiny." Her finger stabbed the air. "It's just love. Shifters fall in love, just like people do, and they make the same mistakes. And after a while, it all breaks down. Disagreements turn into fights. Small concessions become huge compromises. Dreams get thrown away. Look at my mom, or yours, with Dad, for goodness' sake. Look what a mess he made of their lives."

The mess he made of all of our lives, she might as well have added.

"Neither one of our moms was his destined mate," Tina insisted.

"No, they were just a couple of women hopelessly in love. Blind until it was too late." Carly's voice was laced with bitterness. Disappointment. Determination not to make the same mistake. "Look, guys can be a lot of fun. But destined mates are a myth. Old-fashioned bullshit used to keep women in their place." She crossed her arms in silent defiance.

"No one's saying you have to mate," Tina murmured.

She snorted. "A damn good thing, too. I don't want a man. Don't need a man."

Well, I do. Tina needed a man, or she'd go insane. Correction—a man of her own. Not her two brothers, not the dozen well-meaning other males in her pack. Her own man.

Rick.

"I really don't see why any woman would want to mate."

"Well, I can't mate with him, so it's all academic anyway," Tina snapped.

"Why is it..." Carly trailed off. "Wait. Is Dad pulling one of his bullshit moves and trying to set you up with someone else?"

She snorted. Given her age, her dad would probably be happy to see her mated to just about any man in any pack. He'd certainly made his fair share of suggestions—often bluntly and in the most mortifying public situations—on suitable mates. He'd probably accept just about any he-wolf for her. But a human? Never.

Lately, though, her father had done an about-face, apparently having decided there were advantages to having a spinster daughter, married to ranch duties instead of a man.

She shook her head, avoiding Carly's gaze. "My mate..." She had to stop there, because her heart ached just from hearing the words uttered aloud for the first time. *My mate.* Her wolf purred, but her human side wailed. How could destiny be so cruel? "He's human. I can't."

They drove on in silence, climbing higher and higher through the desert. Too high for the scarecrow-shaped saguaro cactus that dotted the city and its surroundings. High-altitude ranch country stretched uninterrupted in both directions, on and on to the purple-blue line of mountains beyond. There were days when the desert seemed chock-full of hidden gems, just waiting to be discovered. Other times it just looked barren. Empty. Hopeless.

"I don't get it." Carly gestured. "You believe in destined mates, but you won't mate him. Some logic."

"He's human. A mating bite could kill him."

"Heather is human. She didn't die."

"Heather's a woman."

"So?"

"It's different."

"Bullshit."

"It isn't!" Tina thumped the steering wheel. "Men fight the change more. They hardly ever survive. You know what they say. The stronger the man, the more his body will resist."

Carly waved an unimpressed hand. "Old wives' tales."

"It's a fact. A fact, Carly!" She was almost yelling now, but she didn't care. "Kyle nearly died from the change. His body fought it that hard. And my mate..." There it was again, the hitch in her voice when she said it. *My mate.* "He's strong. Maybe even stronger than Kyle. He wouldn't make it."

"If destiny wanted him to be yours," Carly argued, "he ought to be fine, right?"

"And if destiny is just messing around?"

A long silence stretched while they avoided each other's eyes. When Carly finally whispered, her face was turned to the open plains.

"Then he'll die."

Chapter Nineteen

Rick turned the shower head to cold and let that pound his body for a little while. He needed it, bad. Not just to cleanse the layers of sweat stuck to his skin at the end of a hard working day, but to settle down that hard-on he got just thinking about Tina.

"So you'll come?" he'd asked—just about begged—into the phone.

"Rick. . ." Tina's voice wavered. So full of want, so full of frustration.

"Come. Please." He'd have gotten down on his knees if it would have helped. "Please come."

He had to strain to hear her answer. But even as a whisper, it made his heart soar. "I'll come."

Finally, finally, he'd get to see her again. The day had seemed as torturously long as the last seven years, and spending last night with her had only doubled his need for her.

About an hour after he called her, he'd been checking the roof tiles on the Seymours' house when his phone beeped with a text from Tina, and even that made his heart beat faster. Yes, he brought his phone up there with him, just in case she called.

Dress code for dinner?

He sat perched up there like a lonely hawk and studied the view. Wiped the sweat off his brow and thought. Now, shoot. He still hadn't made his mind up where to take her. But then a fresh breeze wafted out of the north, and he knew. He texted back.

Best riding boots, worst jeans.

That was three hours ago; he'd had just enough time to set things up. He cooked the dinner he'd feed her afterward, cleaned himself up, and headed down to the barn.

"Easy, Blue," he murmured to Henry's aging horse. The horse was brown, but old Henry had named all his horses Blue after a roan he'd owned way back when. Henry named all his horses Blue and all his dogs Tex. The color of the horses varied, but the dogs were always look-alike versions of the same spotted mutt.

Poor old Blue hadn't been ridden in years, and even though he was a little stiff in the knees, he was keen as anything to get out in the desert again. A little like Rick. Blue pranced in place, excited and nervous as a colt, as if this was his big chance.

Again, a little like Rick.

"Easy," he murmured, easing the saddle over the horse's back.

Blue nickered and butted Rick's leg in anticipation. *Let's go.*

He laughed, and that felt good. Good to have someone on this ranch to laugh with, even if it was just a horse.

"Hang on, now. Gotta get your date ready, too. Ready, Star?"

Star was Lucy's latest ride, a palomino that was still young and sprightly enough to make a guy think twice about handing her reins over to just anyone, especially since she hadn't been ridden in years. But he wasn't handing the reins over to just anyone. Tina could ride the wildest, craziest thing on four feet.

He chuckled at himself. If it were just anyone, he wouldn't be heading out on a sunset ride. Not for a ride, not for the dinner he had planned for after, not for any of the rest. He'd spent an hour brushing those horses, getting their coats to shine like they were show ponies and not a couple of working-class quarter horses.

But it worked. They looked... nice. He ran a hand down his shirt, wishing he'd had someone to double check him the same way. His twenty days were counting down, and he had to make this date count.

He was readjusting the corner of Star's saddle blanket for the fifth or sixth time when Tina pulled up in that silver Corolla of hers and stepped out. Best riding boots. Worst jeans. She'd look like a million bucks no matter what she wore.

He ran a nervous hand over his shirt and strode over, trying not to run. Forcing himself to keep his hands at his sides and not sweep her into his arms and kiss her senseless like every muscle in his body wanted to do.

"Hello, Tina."

He did kiss her, though, because there was no holding *that* back. Smack on the mouth with his hands cupping her face and his feet planted firmly so there'd be no dumb ideas about letting his body drift closer, closer...

He yanked himself back just as her knees started to buckle. Much as he'd like to carry her up to the apartment and start last night all over again, he did have the horses saddled. That, and he really didn't want to take Tina up to his bed.

At least not yet.

He wanted a magical evening, for her and for him. He wanted to listen to her laugh, to see her smile. To watch the stars come out, one by one, and let the feeling of home seep back into his bones.

"Let me guess," Tina said when he finally waved toward their mounts. "That one is Blue."

The laugh that escaped his lips carried his worries away. A laugh of relief because he'd never have to explain that joke to Tina. He'd never have to explain what the grandfather clock meant to this place, or why old Lucy's garden deserved to be revived. Tina just knew. She knew the ranch. She knew him. The real him.

He handed her the reins but kept his fingers over hers. "This one's Star."

She nodded. "Lucy's horse."

See? All the important things, Tina knew.

"Can I leave my purse here? I'm guessing I don't exactly need my phone on this ride."

"Not exactly." He smiled back. No interruptions. Not tonight.

109

He nodded to a shelf, did a last saddle check, and they mounted up. He pointed Blue north and set off at an easy walk. Tina rode beside him, wearing a grin a mile wide. She looked left, right, up, and down, marveling in every view.

She sighed. "I haven't had the chance to get out riding in... well, a long time."

"Me, neither." It had been years. But it felt good to be out. Really good.

For Tina, too. She looked happier, freer than she had when she'd first driven up.

"I think Blue has a crush on Star." She smiled, glancing his way.

"And how do you know that?"

"He follows her with his eyes, his ears, his nose. Every move she makes, he follows along."

A little like I'm doing with you. "I guess he does," Rick said quietly. "I guess he does."

They rode over the rise, skirting the hill where the cemetery lay, and Rick had the craziest image of old Henry and Lucy, arm in arm up there, waving him and Tina off, saying, *Have a good time.* His dad and mom were there, too, standing side by side, smiling and shooing them off like a couple of kids at a fair.

And just like that, the stakes on this one night tripled. Quadrupled. Multiplied exponentially until he had to do like he'd done a thousand times at bat: take a deep breath and pretend it was just a game he was playing and not something much, much bigger than that.

"So beautiful," Tina murmured.

"Yeah," he managed, watching her hair sway with every step Star took. "Beautiful."

She smiled at a firefly. Pointed at a stand of purple twinevine. Tilted her head back and took in the deepening brushfire color of the sky.

Time switched off, stripping away centuries, scraping away the tension. The dusky fragrance of a thousand desert flowers carried on the wind.

"Beautiful," she murmured when they paused at the edge of the mesa. Together, they looked over a thousand square miles of home, a mile-high sky of clean desert air.

Rick closed his eyes, drinking it all in. Just the two of them and the horses and the dog that trotted in and out of sight. Not another soul as far as he could see.

Then Blue nickered and Star whinnied. *Time to get moving, boss.*

"That way." He pointed to the track that wound into a grove of cottonwood.

"That way?" Tina's eyes grew wide, because she knew just where he meant.

"Spring Hollow." He nodded. Grand as the view up here was, he needed someplace smaller, lusher... more intimate to share with her.

"Spring Hollow," she echoed, biting her lip.

He let Blue lead the way and thanked every saint in heaven when the sound of Star's hooves followed, because it meant that Tina wasn't galloping away from the past, but heading back in to explore it with him.

Spring Hollow. The most beautiful corner of the ranch. Well, sort of a corner of the ranch, because Lucy Seymour had deeded it to the state when she died. One of her crazier last wishes, like naming him manager of the ranch. It was a peaceful little pocket of land where a fresh spring bounced and gurgled, feeding a hundred shady trees. A place that didn't belong to the ranch or the state or anyone else. More like it belonged to God or Mother Nature or some powerful force a guy like him couldn't begin to comprehend. All he knew was how perfect it was.

"Rick..."

He turned and looked at Tina, praying she wouldn't protest.

"It's... it's..." She fumbled with words.

Home? Beautiful? Ours for tonight?

"It's just like I remember."

Yeah, just like he remembered, too. The rustle of leaves, the babbling stream—sounds, smells, sights you didn't get in the open desert. Just in a secret hideaway like this.

Blue whisked his tail and descended the overgrown trail with Star right on his heels. Trees arched overhead, forming a cathedral of the woods: a hushed, almost spiritual place. Rick dismounted, led his horse to drink, then tied the reins to a branch and looked at Tina.

An all-or-nothing moment, because she was still two stories up on Star, chewing her lip. She could turn her tail and hammer away into the sunset, or she could slide out of the saddle and let him lead her to their special place. The spot on the boulders where they'd first kissed, first touched, first made love, all those years ago.

Tina looked at him, and he could feel the ache in her as clearly as he felt in himself.

Please, he wanted to whisper. *Please, Tina. Trust me. Trust yourself.*

Her eyes flashed, telling him she knew perfectly well he wasn't leading her into the past so much as leading her into a future.

She waited so long, he was tempted to hang his head and let her go, except he couldn't, because he'd never, ever give up on Tina. Maybe he'd have to give her an extra twenty days to decide. Maybe he'd wait forever. Maybe all he had to do was—

Tina shifted, stood in her stirrups, and threw a leg over Star. Slid to the ground in one easy glide and, without another second's hesitation, stepped right over to him.

She was shaking her head like she was sure she was crazy, but she kissed him all the same. Kissed him with dry, craving lips that opened and closed as if she was whispering at the same time. Praying maybe. Telling him how crazy *he* was.

She didn't make a sound, though. Just kissed. Kissed and kissed without a breath in between, one hand still gripping Star's reins like it'd be safer not to let go, and the other hand hugging him close. He threaded his fingers through her hair and hung on as emotions cascaded through those quietly whispering lips. Fear. Doubt. Hope. Desire. Each one slowly melting into the next until there was only one left.

Love.

"I love you, Rick." He could swear he heard her think it—twice, in fact—before she said it, though by then it didn't matter any more because she really had said it out loud. "I love you. I missed you. I want you."

He kept waiting for the *but*. Kept holding his breath, waiting for the other shoe to drop.

She didn't say it, though he could feel it hanging in the air along with the rising moon. Her starved kisses continued until she paused long enough to lead him over to the flat red rocks by the stream. She lunged into a kiss then settled on his lap and started working down the buttons of his shirt.

"Why?" He managed to get out. His hands swept over her back, cupped her rear, pulled her closer. "Why did we ever part?"

A rhetorical question, really, although Tina hid her face in his shoulder and mumbled a reply. "I always wanted you. I only wanted you."

"Then why?"

She shook her head. "Rick, I just want to think about now. I just want tonight."

A little voice inside started screaming, *No! No! No!* "I want more." *I want everything.*

Her lower lip wavered between a kiss and a word. Then she blinked and looked at him with those dark, tragic eyes. "I want more, too. I want it more than anything. I just..."

There was no *just*. There couldn't be.

She shook her head hopelessly, and he could see the war in her eyes.

Just when he thought he'd lost, her eyes darkened. Sparked a little and then glowed. It must have been the reflection from the moon and the sunset, filtering through the trees, but damn, her eyes really seemed to glow. And just like that, she was wild for him. Kissing, wet and deep and hard. Raking her nails over his back and straddling him, pushing him back on the rock at the same time. Her fingers tugged his shirt from where it had been tucked into his jeans. It was as if a wild thing had jumped out of a caged part of her soul and taken over the controls. A wild thing that lit every last one of his nerves so that he was on fire, too.

She growled into the next kiss, and the points of her teeth nipped his lips. *I want you. No more talking. I want us.*

Now he was imagining her voice in his head.

She worked his zipper down, then his jeans, and yanked off his shirt. He stripped her, layer by layer, holding his breath the whole time. Tina was that beautiful, that perfect. His. When she slid down over him, she tilted her head back and moaned. Then she started rocking, and all he could do was grip her hips and pump and marvel at the woman doing this to him. Maybe even growl a little on the side, because there was a feral edge to this he'd never experienced before. His bare ass was cold on the rock, but Tina was an inferno, all friction and hunger and sheer feminine power. Her cries joined the steady hum of cicadas, the whisper of the brook, and it all roared in his ears. Like the brook wasn't a brook but a gushing river. Like the hollow was a concert hall with a string orchestra playing full blast. Everything swelled beyond real-life proportions. Beyond pleasure, right up to the razor's edge of a blissful kind of pain.

Mine! Mine! Mine! Her body screamed the word with every tiny gesture, every heavy moan.

Mine. If Tina allowed herself to think it, damn it, so could he. *Mine.* She was his, all his.

His whole body shuddered when he came, and Tina cried out at exactly the same time. She grabbed his shoulders, convulsing, and murmured incomprehensible sounds. Then she slumped over him, and all he could think about was holding her. Holding her forever and never, ever letting go.

She spent a long time panting into his shoulder before slowly pulling herself together. The sun was over the horizon, and night had set in, but when she looked up, the glow was still in her eyes.

He pressed his lips to her collarbone. There was nothing he could say to capture what he felt. Nothing either of them could do to make this more perfect.

"Rick," she whispered, nuzzling him the way only she could. Scrubbing her chin against his skin like she wanted part of him to rub off on her. "Rick..."

Perfect. Absolutely perfect. A dream.

Until a split second later, when her whole body went stiff and her head popped up. He could swear her ears flicked.

"What—?" He'd barely started when an ear-splitting howl cut into the night. A hellish cry of a tortured creature bent on revenge.

Chapter Twenty

Rick could have pulled a plug on the soundtrack of the hollow, it went quiet that fast. Then it roared back to life with crazed whinnies from the horses and the puff of Tina's panicked breath.

Aaaaaarrroooo... The creature howled from somewhere far away, but still much, much too close.

Not a coyote. Not even a wolf like the ones Rick had heard as a kid. Something canine and dangerous but somehow different.

Blue reared up and clawed against empty air, whinnying in alarm.

Tina sprang off his lap. "Hell. How—" Whatever she was saying, it was urgent. Alarmed.

Every hair on his neck stood straight up, every muscle tensed. He had no idea what creature made a sound like that. The frightening thing was that Tina seemed to know exactly what it was, and she was scared stiff.

"Quick, quick!" She tossed his jeans at him and rushed to pull on her clothes in record time. She hissed at the horses, and they went silent instantly, though their hooves tore at the ground. Their nostrils were huge, their eyes panicked. Whatever evil was afoot had them ready to flee.

Now. Fast. Far. The urgent message coursed through his veins.

"Go!" Tina urged as she untied Star and leaped into the saddle. "Go!"

Rick barely had a foot in the stirrup when Blue shot off, and it was all he could do was throw a leg over the saddle and hang on, ducking low over Blue's mane as branches thwacked him from all sides. God, what was going on? The whole desert was on red alert, and him, too.

A wild minute of bushwhacking later, they shot out into the open and thundered across the desert, heading home. Blue didn't need any urging; more like he needed to be held back before he stumbled and broke a leg. He galloped at a pace no aging horse should attempt, straining for another gear.

"Easy, boy." Rick tried calming the horse, but his voice was uneven, unconvincing. Whatever was out there was evil. He could feel it in his bones.

Three lengths ahead, Tina leaned so low over Star's neck that she was practically part of the horse. Her dark hair streamed back and whipped wildly with the mare's pale mane, the very picture of a goddess of the wind or the sky. Or maybe even a goddess of battle, because when Tina glanced back, her face was fierce, her eyes flashing as if she were planning to rally the troops and go hunt down whatever it was that pumped terror into the desert that night.

The howls continued. From the direction of Dead Horse Bluff, maybe? He couldn't tell, not at full gallop and with the desert screeching full-on panic in his ears.

They thundered over a rise until the ranch came into view, and the only thought in his mind was to race for the barn and bolt every door. To grab Tina, carry her into the loft, and stand two steps in front of her on guard. Maybe even grab a shotgun along the way, or a pitchfork, or whatever he could grab, and fight to the death if it meant she'd survive.

One howl oughtn't do that to a man who'd walked some mean city streets, but it did. That howl was ghostly. Evil. Devilish, even.

They thundered down the hill, past the outer paddocks, past the empty house and right through the open barn door, ducking to clear their heads. The horses scrambled to a halt, trembling. Their nostrils flared and they skittered in place, hooves clawing the dirt, while he and Tina leaped to the ground and rushed for the door. He had it nearly all the way shut when Tina stopped and slid halfway out.

"What—?"

118

"I have to go."

"Go?" With that thing out there? Was she nuts?

But Tina wasn't nuts. She was the goddess of the wind, or something very close. "I have to go."

"Tina, you can't—"

She put a hand on his arm, and for a split second, everything calmed down. The roaring in his ears, the sense of urgency, the fear. Everything but the instinct to protect.

"Trust me, I have to go."

Any other woman, he'd have pulled back into the barn because it was crazy, absolutely crazy to drive out into that haunted night. His father had had just enough pagan in him to believe in ghosts and demons, and Rick believed, too. He couldn't not believe, hearing the otherworldliness in the howl that had split the night.

A howl that had gone quiet by now, but who knew when it might pipe up again, or where?

Tex, the dog, came hurtling in a minute behind the horses, tail tucked so far between his legs it was a wonder the animal didn't trip. He shot right into his crate in a corner and huddled there, panting and wild-eyed.

"I have to go." Tina's voice cracked. If her mind was made up, her heart sure didn't agree. He could see duty wrestle with desire in there. But she had the look of a warrior committed to battle, and it was pointless to stop her.

So he didn't try. He just grabbed his keys and followed her into the night.

"What are you doing?" she cried.

"I'm going with you."

"Rick, no—"

He figured she'd protest, but if she was having her way, he was having his. "I'll follow you in my truck until you're safe at home."

"How will I know you get safely home?" she protested.

Something in him twinged. His Amazon thought she had to protect him when it was the other way around.

"I will get home safely. I'll be waiting for you. Tomorrow."

I'll wait for you forever, he nearly added.

If he could freeze the look on her face... That *I love you, you idiot* look he'd be happy to catch glimpses of for the next fifty or sixty years.

I love you, my princess. He formed the words in his mind and pushed them into the night, maybe hoping she'd catch a whisper of them in the wind.

Tina didn't move. Didn't blink. But her nostrils flared just a tiny bit. Enough to make him wonder if maybe—

"Let's go," she murmured, turning on her heel.

And just like that, they headed back into the night. Tina drove her little hatchback the way she'd ridden Star: hard and fast, with Rick hot on her tail in his truck, working all eight cylinders mercilessly. He followed her eight miles, all the way to the gate of Twin Moon Ranch, where they rolled to a stop.

Tina looked up at him, ducking to see past the frame of the cab. "Be careful. Stay inside."

Exactly what he was about to tell her.

"Tina..."

"I'll call you tomorrow." She was a woman on a mission, and his time was up.

It was going to kill him to turn and drive away now, but the gate was like a trench line, and the bridge across the dry creek bed in front of him marked no man's land. He'd never stepped foot on Twin Moon Ranch. He wondered if he ever would.

The only part of the picture he could swallow was the fact that she had two tough-ass brothers, a bull of a father, and God knew how many burly ranch hands to keep her safe on the other side of that line. Back on Seymour Ranch, it was just him. Him and a washed-up cowboy who'd gone out drinking for the night. So yeah, Twin Moon was a better place for her to be tonight.

Even so, it took everything he had to let her go. "You be careful."

"You, too."

She nodded, and he nodded, and that was it. The end of a nearly perfect night.

He watched her go, and the desert went silent except for the muffled howl coming from his heart.

Chapter Twenty-One

"Hell of a night," Kyle grunted, dropping to a bench outside the council house.

"Damnedest thing." Cody nodded, and even he looked serious and drawn.

"Not a sign..." Kyle muttered, kicking at the ground.

"Not a trace." Cody shook his head.

Only that terrible howling that sent a shiver through Tina's nerves.

The sun was rising, and most of the pack was gathered in front of the council house, weary to the bone. They'd been out all night tracking the hellhound in groups of three and four, to no avail.

"That sound came from the mesa," Cody murmured.

"We heard it from the creek," Rae said, looking at Zack.

"Farther west, I thought," her mate said.

The only one who'd actually seen it was Beth, the librarian, who trembled while describing the glowing red eyes. Just a glimpse, and then it had taken off.

"Where? Where did it go?"

Beth shook her head hopelessly. "I don't know."

Ty stalked back and forth, practically spitting fire, and even Lana couldn't calm him down. She looked haggard too, after a long night on watch. A night of confusion, because no one could pin down where the howls had come from.

"Goddamn ghost hound," Ty cursed. "What do the coyotes say?"

Zack looked grim. He and Rae had probably covered more ground than anyone else, and it showed. His eyes were hollow, his back stooped. "Atsa's pack reported the same thing: it was everywhere, it was nowhere."

"Fucking hellhound has to be somewhere," Ty grunted. He clenched his fists, and Tina could read the rest on his mind. *And when I find it, I will rip it limb from limb.*

But even her brother would have a hard time doing that alone. How many might die, she wondered, trying to take the demon down? Who would pay the ultimate price?

Tina studied the colors seeping slowly out of the sky as the sun rose higher. It was a dawn she'd been hoping to wake up to in a different place. Hoping to find a beautiful new day after a beautiful night.

You should listen to me more often, her wolf murmured.

She could still feel Rick's gentle touch. See his chocolate eyes. Hear his thoughts in her head. And if that didn't prove that he was her destined mate, nothing would.

Except it also proved how careless she'd been. What if the hellhound had come down to Spring Hollow? What if it had attacked? Rick would be dead, and if she somehow survived, she'd have to live with the guilt for the rest of her life.

"If that hound snuck on to the ranch while we were out searching..." Carly murmured the unspeakable, and Tina's stomach lurched.

If that had happened while she was away... If lives had been lost while she was off gallivanting with a human she had no right dragging into her world... She paled, imagining a dozen horrifying scenarios. Zack and Rae, caught out on the ranch border, fighting to the death, side by side, refusing to give an inch. Or Kyle and Stef, battling the hellhound at the door to their outlying home, desperate to save their child. Ty and Cody would come to help, but Lana and Heather would have to stay back to watch their kids, and if the hellhound stole around the back...

Any of that could have happened last night, and she wouldn't have been there to help because she'd only been thinking about herself.

Our mate! Thinking about our mate! her wolf insisted.

He's not our mate! she screamed back. *He never will be!*

Her gut twisted harder still, but her mind was made up. The pack had to come first. The pack always came first.

"What now?" Carly asked.

Everyone looked to Ty, who looked to Zack. "What do you think?"

Zack scraped a hand through his hair. "It'll have gone underground," he said. "For now."

For now?

"Gone away?" Lana's voice was scratchy with doubt.

"Could be, or. . . " Zack murmured.

Everyone leaned closer to catch his low voice.

"Could be, the hellhound just had his first look at the valley last night. If it decides to stay put, we have big trouble."

"And if it decides to move on?" Carly tried.

"Then somebody else will have big trouble," Rae sighed.

That was the thing. The hellhound could attack anywhere, anytime, and even a pack as strong as Twin Moon was vulnerable. The children. The elderly. Even the most powerful wolf—the likes of Ty or Cody or Kyle—could only hope to survive a hellhound fight with superior numbers and a coordinated attack.

Tina caught herself staring south, in the direction of Seymour Ranch. She dragged her eyes away with an effort and focused on the brand hanging above the ranch gate instead. Two circles overlapping by a third swung in the breeze. Twin Moon Ranch. This was her home. This was her place to defend.

But what about our mate? The wolf clawed at her insides

She kicked it heartlessly into the cellar of her soul and slammed the door shut with a crash. A crash that echoed in her heart, because another door slammed there at the same time.

She couldn't think about herself at a time like this. Couldn't! Only about her pack.

"Right," Ty barked.

Everyone's ears perked to attention as he started issuing orders. Some of the wolves were sent home to rest while others continued the search. Zack and Rae nodded and trotted grimly to the west, where they would rendezvous with a group of coyotes.

"Like I can get any sleep with a hellhound out," Cody muttered.

"I need you fresh to take over later," Ty muttered, unyielding.

Cody glanced at Tina and rolled his eyes. *Like Ty will ever take a break.*

Tina shrugged. *At least he's trying to delegate some things. He can't do this alone.*

He won't, she assured him. *We'll do it together.*

Cody managed a little smile before stumbling off on weary feet.

The council house became a command post, with wolves scurrying in and out. Tina stayed all day, coordinating the details to the bolder brush strokes of Ty's overall plan. He and Kyle bent over maps, considered distances, grumbled about the terrain. Lana popped in and out from her office across the way where she headed up communications with allied packs.

"Anything new?" Ty asked the fourth or fifth time Lana strode in.

She shook her head. "Westend pack in Nevada hasn't seen a thing. No unusual reports from my contacts around the state, either..."

When Ty turned away, Lana looked straight at Tina and tilted her head toward the door. *There is one thing,* she whispered into Tina's mind.

Nerves pinged through Tina's body like overtight guitar strings as she followed Lana outside.

Lana pulled a sheet of paper from her pocket and opened it slowly. Excruciatingly slowly.

"What? What is it?" Tina's blood pressure jumped.

Lana exhaled slowly before starting. "This just came in." She shook her head. "It isn't about the hellhound. It's about Seymour Ranch."

Tina glanced at the paper. *Department of Water Resources,* said the header, next to the state crest.

"Remember the rumor about drilling for more water?"

How could she forget?

"Seymour Ranch filed the request. Yesterday."

Tina snatched the sheet out of Lana's hand. Yesterday? Yesterday she'd woken up with Rick, then hurried to pick Carly up from the airport. A few hours later, she'd gone to meet Rick again.

Hours he'd filled with more than just prettying up the horses for her, apparently.

There's no plan to draw more water. I swear there isn't. Rick's exact words to her, two days ago, when they'd looked over the books.

He swore to her face.

She stared at the paper, and there it all was. Dated, signed, delivered. *Seymour Ranch proposal to increase output from Cameron aquifer, as per state regulation 45-596...*

Her blood stood still.

Every guy is out to use women, in his own way. That's what Carly said by way of goodbye the day before. Her warning echoed in Tina's mind. *What if this guy is using you, Tina? You ever consider that?*

Of course she'd considered that—and promptly dismissed it. Why would Rick use her?

You're the manager of one the biggest ranches in Arizona. Any number of guys would love to get into your pants. A, because you're pretty fucking gorgeous, and B, because who knows what information or favors he might win along the way?

Rick didn't need information. He didn't need favors.

Every guy uses women in his own way.

For a sunny Californian, her sister had an awfully bitter streak.

Tina had dismissed the suggestion at the time, but now...

There's no plan to draw more water. I swear there isn't. Rick had said that to her face.

God, what if Carly was right?

I swear... Rick had said. He swore! He promised.

She looked back at the paper, feeling sick.

How could he?

She was about to spin on her heel and stamp to her car, purple with rage, when her wolf roared inside. *How could you doubt him?*

He lied!

Our mate would never lie to us!

He lied! He... She couldn't quite summon the willpower to continue.

"Um, Tina?" Lana tilted her head. A breath of wind rustled the paper in her hand.

Our mate would never lie! her wolf raged on.

She snatched the paper out of Lana's hand and studied it.

"Tina, what is it?"

Tina barely heard; all her concentration was on the fax. Would Rick really have lied to her?

Our mate wouldn't lie! her wolf growled.

Tina squinted at Rick's signature at the bottom of the sheet. Held the paper closer with shaking hands.

"Tina, what is it?"

She forced herself to steady the sheet with both hands. Closed her eyes. Recalled the ledgers in the Seymour office. The writing had changed over time, going from Henry's years of record-keeping to a brief period of Lucy's and finally Dale's blocky print.

Her eyes snapped open and scrutinized the form. Everything was filled in by that same brutish hand, right down to the forged signature.

See? Our mate would never lie!

Her mind spun. Was Dale working behind Rick's back? She liked that scenario a hell of a lot better than Rick lying to her.

For a second, she nearly rejoiced, but then the implications set in. What else might Dale be up to? And did Rick even suspect?

Her stomach lurched as she recalled some of the entries in the ledgers. Dynamite. The note with the contact number for... what was it again?

"Danielson... Davidson..." She looked up at Lana. "Danielson Resources? Davidson? Do you know them?"

128

Lana scowled. "Davidson Resources. A mining company that just won't quit. What does that have to do with—" Her head whipped around to the council house, where Ty was beckoning her with a question. "Sorry. I'll be right back."

Lana strode off, leaving Tina alone with the fax and her thoughts.

Dale. Water rights. Mining company.

Dale working behind Rick's back.

Her wolf started snarling inside. *Let's get Rae and Lana and go snap Dale's cheating neck.*

Tempted. She was sorely tempted. But her packmates were busy with far more urgent matters at the moment.

Fine. Let's you and me go snap Dale's neck.

That plan, she liked. She walked the first two steps to her car. Jogged the next three, and flat-out sprinted the last few. Then she peeled out of the driveway and out under the ranch gate.

Chapter Twenty-Two

Rick thought the night was bad enough: wondering about that beastly howl, worrying about Tina. But the day was proving just as bad. Not just waking up alone on a morning that should have started with Tina curled next to him, but waiting for a call.

She'd promised to phone him. So why didn't she? What was taking so long?

He paced and paced and paced with that scrappy mutt Tex at his heels the whole time. The dog shadowed him everywhere, badly spooked by the beast in the night.

Well, at least there was that. His crazy night had brought him two new friends: a brown horse named Blue and a mutt called Tex. Now if only he could persuade Tina to join his oddball team...

He had to smile a little at that. From the San Diego Padres to the scrappy crew at Seymour Ranch. A team with a lot of promise, if only he could get key players on board.

"Twenty days," he sighed to the dog, who looked up with sympathetic eyes. "Ten down, ten to go."

Tex looked at him as if to say, *And then what?*

A good thing dogs didn't speak, because Rick didn't have an answer for that one. "Just gotta get through the first twenty, Tex. That's the rule."

He couldn't stand around fretting all day, but he couldn't tear himself away from the house, because what if Tina called the land-line and not his cell phone? So he set about weeding the second half of Lucy's garden while the dog snoozed in the shade nearby. Every weed he plucked brought thoughts of Dale, and every tenacious flower hidden in the mess carried images of Tina. What was she doing? What was going on at Twin Moon Ranch?

Dale, for his part, seemed to have returned more cantankerous than ever from his last drinking spree. He wheezed and cursed and finally disappeared into the barn, all without any mention of the strange howling. Dale had eventually driven off on some errand at noon, and Rick went right on weeding and dreaming about the team he'd form at Seymour Ranch if he could. Get rid of Dale and hire a few new hands. Find a couple of young rookies who were eager to learn, plus a couple of experienced hands with a strong work ethic to guide them. He'd need someone familiar with those Heritage breed steer Henry had been so keen to try out, too. And once the ranch was back on its feet, he and Tina could...

Could what? When? Would she ever come around?

A raven cawed, and the sound echoed over the nearly deserted ranch. Rick wiped the sweat from his brow and sighed. Yeah, he had a lot of work ahead of him yet.

The work, he didn't mind. It was the wait that killed him. Waiting patiently while he sowed the seeds for his vision, and waiting for Tina's call.

When the phone rang, it was with a text tone and not the chime of a live call, but he jumped for it all the same. Exhaled in relief to see it was from her. He smiled at the screen, clicked to open the message, and promptly cursed.

The dog jumped to its feet as Rick reread it and cursed again.

Must talk to you. Urgent! Meet at Diablo Mine. Hurry!

Of all the messages he'd imagined Tina writing, that sure wasn't it. But it was her number, all right.

Why would Tina want to meet him at Diablo Mine and not at the ranch? A thousand possible scenarios ran through his mind as he fired up his pickup and set off on the drive. He didn't notice the dog trying to follow until about a mile down the road, when he caught a glimpse of the dejected mutt panting wildly in the rearview mirror. He was about to pull over to wait, but by then Tex had given up, so he drove on alone. No time to wait now, because his veins were itching with urgency. More and more with every mile of the long and lonely road up into the hills. Something was wrong.

The whole thing felt strange. Tina, texting but not calling? Meeting him at a place like this?

He parked the car at the top of Dead Horse Bluff, his least favorite place in the world, and looked around. Nothing. Nobody. He sat behind the wheel, stroking a thumb against his chest for a good minute after shutting the engine off.

Not a thing, except maybe buzzards and ghosts.

He got out and eyed the cliff. Wondered for the hundredth time about his father's death. Wondered why Tina would ever meet him in a godforsaken place like this.

Maybe she was still on her way. He looked around, hoping to see a plume of rising dust that signaled the approach of a car on these back roads. But there was nothing. Nothing but him, a thousand square miles of slumbering desert, and that leaden feeling in his gut.

Must talk to you. Urgent!

His eyes wandered to the boarded-up entrance to the mine, and he did a double take. The couple of old boards that had blocked the mine entrance lay discarded on the ground, and a black hole yawned.

Why was the mine open?

His stride grew longer, more urgent, then shortened again as he approached the mine.

Never go near there, you understand? It's a bad, bad place. His father's warnings rang in his ears.

Would Tina venture in there? Would she dare?

"Hello?" he called quietly into the darkness.

-ello... -llo, came the ghostly echo.

He listened. Nothing. "Tina?"

-ina... -ina...

A shiver rippled down his spine.

No. No way would Tina venture down there. Why would she? Why would anyone come to this godforsaken place? The only person who'd been up here lately was Dale and—

His thoughts screeched to a halt, spinning wildly. So wildly, he didn't hear the footsteps behind him before it was too late.

"Looking for someone?"

He spun and there on his blind side was Dale. Dale and a double-barreled shotgun, pointed at his chest.

Dale spat a wad of tobacco on the ground and grinned. A twisted, ugly grin of blackened teeth behind cracked lips.

"Dale," Rick grunted, slowly raising his hands.

"No one up here but you, me, and the crows," Dale chuckled.

Rick held perfectly still, though his eyes darted around.

"Looking for this?" Dale held out a phone. Tina's phone. How did he get his hands on that?

Rick stared at him. Dale sent the text? Then where was Tina?

The panic must have been written on his face, because Dale laughed. "Nah, she ain't here. But maybe I ought to invite her up here later. Yeah, that's a good idea. I could use *your* phone for that..." Rick could see the gears spinning in Dale's head as the wicked smile stretched. "Maybe I'll invite the little lady up here to peek over the edge of the cliff. What do you think about that?"

Rick froze at the triumphant tone in the man's voice.

Dale's smile turned into a sneer. "Accidents do happen, you know."

Dale might as well have run cold steel through Rick's gut.

"You did it. You killed my father." His voice was the only thing that felt steady right now. Why would anyone want that gentle soul dead?

Dale shrugged. "Not my fault he came snooping around here."

The cold air of the mine tickled Rick's back as his mind raced. So many thoughts and emotions at one time, it was all a flash of colors. Blazing red was for the rage shaking his bones. The sinking black hole in his gut was grief. And the ivory blur was fear. Not for himself, but for Tina. What if Dale really did lure her up here?

"You killed my father over some leftover gold?" Who would do such a thing?

Dale cackled. "Like this mine's got any gold that's worth my time."

Worth his time? How much did Dale reckon a washed-up cowboy's time was worth?

Dale worked up a glob of phlegm and spat before ranting on. "This is why you're such a shitty manager. Don't know nothing about the value of the land. The land *under* this ranch."

Rick studied Dale. There was that water drilling issue the Hawthornes were so worried about. Was Dale behind that, too? "You killed my father over water rights?"

Dale grimaced. "Water! You think this is about water? Not even his life was worth that little."

The only thing that kept Rick from charging and throttling the man was the rifle pointed at his chest.

The barrel swung briefly toward the mine shaft then back at Rick. "The water is just the start. Uranium is where the big money is."

Rick froze. There'd been talk of uranium among local ranchers for years, but the Seymours had always been dead set against it.

Don't you know what terrible things uranium is used for? Lucy used to protest, pressing a hand against her chest.

The Seymours had been strong enough to resist trading their morals for big money. Dale, on the other hand...

The older man's face twisted into a frown. "Back up." He jerked the barrel of the gun. "Back up."

Rick didn't have much choice but to pick his way backward. Slowly, while his mind raced to come up with some survival plan. Would Dale really shoot him? The answer was in the man's bloodshot eyes. Rick had heard that murder was easier the second time around. And if he was the second, the third time would be even easier, and that would be Tina.

He shook his head. *Think! Think!*

Delay. He needed to delay Dale while thinking up some plan.

"What would make my father snoop around here at all?" he asked.

Dale aimed between his eyes. "Just back up."

Another step, and now he was in the shade of the mine entrance. One more, and the outside world was already a tunnel, far, far away. He wondered if his father had overheard a phone call, or maybe caught a glimpse of a map. Asked an innocent question and set off a nightmare.

A nightmare a lot like this. Rick eyed the beams supporting the mine shaft. All of them were hand-hewn timbers from another age. Could he grab one and take a swing at Dale?

Right, and collapse the mine on top of yourself. Try again.

His foot rolled over a loose stone. Maybe that. He wasn't much of a pitcher, but he sure as hell could hurl one of those if he needed to.

"Golden boy thinks he can just waltz back home and take charge," Dale started to rant. "Well, I got news for you. This ranch is mine, and I'm not gonna sit around while you ruin—"

An ungodly moan came up from the depths of the mine. A moan that stretched into a low, continuous growl just like that of the previous night.

Rick's heart rate jumped into triple time as he whipped around to squint into the darkness.

"What the..." Dale muttered.

Shale crunched under Dale's boots as he backed toward daylight.

"Nuh-uh," the foreman jerked the rifle back up when Rick followed. "You stay right there."

The growl deepened and grew nearer. If the beast had been miles down in the maze of darkness before, it felt much closer now. As in, just-around-the-bend close.

Rick stepped toward Dale, ignoring the gun.

"I said—" Dale started. The syllables echoed down the mine, but all Rick heard was the growl. The growl that had just cleared a corner, along with two glowing red eyes. Every nerve in Rick's body stretched to the breaking point as he fought the instinct to flee.

"Shit," Dale blurted, raising the barrel of his shotgun.

Jesus, what had Dale unleashed in reopening this mine?

An engine sounded outside—another vehicle pulling up. It screeched to a stop and a door slammed.

A voice called into the mine. "Rick?"

He could have screamed. Tina. *No! Not here! Not now!*

"Rick?" she called again. He could see her silhouette in the entrance, backlit by the sun.

"Get away, Tina! Get away!"

The angry growl deepened as the beast coiled to spring. Rick could sense it even in the dark. Another horrible bellow sounded, followed by a shuffling, angry step.

Prepare to die, the beast might as well have announced.

Click-click. Dale cocked the rifle.

"Don't!" Rick shouted as the tight-lipped growl became a bared-teeth snarl. Shooting whatever it was seemed about as smart as shooting a charging grizzly.

"Rick!" Tina screamed.

"Don't!" Rick yelled, waving at Dale.

Dale raised the rifle and squinted down the barrel exactly as the beast leaped.

Boom! The rifleshot thundered through the mine.

Rick leaped aside just as searing heat ripped across his shoulder.

"Rick!" Tina screamed.

The beast roared. The beams supporting the roof creaked. Rick flattened himself against a wall as the beast hurtled through his blind spot and out into the daylight.

Another shout rang out. A second thunderbolt of a shot.

Rick staggered to his feet as horrible screams sounded outside as the beast tore into its prey.

Chapter Twenty-Three

The beast had pushed Dale out into the daylight, and Rick had no choice but to stumble along in its wake. Tina was out there, too, and somehow, he had to get her to safety. The fire in his shoulder didn't matter. The beast didn't matter. Only Tina did.

The whole world zoomed down to the light at the end of that mine shaft, and he staggered toward it.

An overhead beam groaned. The roof shook, raining dirt as Rick ran in a crouch.

Dale screamed in a desperate, barely human voice as the beast ripped into his flesh.

"Rick!" Tina's higher voice cried.

Overhead beams screeched in agony as the roof caved in.

Rick shot forward, half an inch ahead of a collapsing beam. His ears filled with the sounds of a hellstorm: crashing timbers, rumbling earth, the tearing of sharp teeth into mortal flesh. Dale screamed horribly, then whimpered, and finally moaned.

Rick's eyes seared in the sudden daylight. The fire in his shoulder flared. Everything blurred, including the grunting, angry shape that must have been the beast, finishing off Dale.

Tina? Where was Tina?

"Rick!" An urgent whisper reached his ears. A thin hand closed around his. "Quick!"

A warm rush filled his veins, because it was Tina, and that meant there was hope. For her, for him. For them.

She yanked him in the direction of her car.

"Tina!" He spun to catch her as she sprawled over one of the discarded planks that should have been boarding up the mine.

The second he pulled her to her feet, everything went silent. Deathly silent. They both froze and turned at the same time.

The beast rose slowly from Dale's limp body. Its muzzle was flecked with blood and foam as if it were rabid, except rabid animals didn't have eyes that glowed in broad daylight. It moved slowly, confidently, honing in on them. Stopping when it located them. Focusing.

Rick's eyes found their focus, too, and he almost wished he hadn't.

"Hellhound," Tina whispered.

Rick just nodded, because even if he'd never believed in the old stories about demons, he sure believed now. It was a wolf, though not quite a wolf, because it was big and black and crooked, and fire blazed in its eyes. Hair stuck out in all directions from a pelt that might have been dragged through a sooty creek.

The hellhound's teeth parted in a bloody grin. The red-stained jaws clacked once. Twice. *You're next.*

If Rick had been alone, he might have panicked. But *next* was fine with him, because it meant Tina might just be spared.

Act! Save her! Fast!

On instinct, he dipped to grab one of the loose pieces of wood. A two-by-four which felt satisfyingly familiar in his hand. He straightened in the same fluid motion and pushed Tina behind him, toward the car. Bared his own teeth at the hellhound, because this wasn't time for calm and cool and rational, the way he'd always stepped up to the plate. Who cared if his shoulder screamed with every movement?

Mine! Rick let his whole body roar the message. He stood, swinging his makeshift club in defiance.

"Rick! Don't!" Tina cried, tugging at his shirt.

He shoved her—really shoved, and it hurt just to think he had to do that to her. But if he didn't, she would die.

"Get to the car," he hissed through clenched teeth. "Lock yourself in."

The beast growled and advanced one carefully measured step.

That's right, you mangy mutt. Rick weighed the two-by-four in his hands. *Come right this way.*

The hellhound's snarls hit a dangerously low pitch as it advanced, step by step.

"Rick, don't!" Tina tried.

He shook his head. "Get to the—"

The rest was garbled, because the hound leaped, hurtling right at his throat, lightning fast.

Good thing he was faster. Rick swung that two-by-four with every muscle in his body, putting his hips into the rotation, plus his shoulders and elbows and everything else, and swung like he'd never swung before. There was a resounding crack and a surprised yelp as the wood connected and the beast crashed into the ground.

Rick had exactly one half-second to feel the triumph before the beast rolled and turned those twin fireballs on him.

You die.

Rick's lungs tightened just a little bit, making his next breath shaky, but he stood his ground. Brought the two-by-four to his shoulder with a taunting little shake that would have rattled the most seasoned pitcher in the league.

The beast roared and jumped again.

He swung, and this time, the crack was louder.

The beast rolled and batted away the broken half of two-by-four that had splintered in Rick's hands.

Shit.

Tina lunged to his side and started pulling him away. With an ear-splitting bellow, the beast sprung. Not at Rick. At Tina, as if the creature knew how to get him where it counted most.

Something roared in Rick's ears—maybe even his own voice—as he dove and pushed her out of the way. He came to a slamming halt against a rock, and his vision blurred and split into two. He saw two Tinas, scrambling to her feet. Two hellhounds, baring a hell of lot of teeth. Four blazing eyes that promised a painful death. Red-stained muzzles still dripping Dale's blood.

It leaped at him, and he threw an arm up in defense. The beast took the target in its jaws and clamped down.

Fireworks rocketed through his body in a flash of pain. One startlingly calm part of his brain calculated that the beast would rip that arm right out of its socket if he didn't do something fast. It'd rip his arm off, then tear out his throat, then go for Tina.

Not happening, he told himself. Just not happening.

A sliver of saliva dropped from the beast's gums, searing his skin like acid. Telling him to give up and give in.

Never giving in.

With a mighty heave, he flipped the hound away and rolled free. Grabbed another piece of wood with his good hand, because the arm bitten by the hellhound hung limp and useless at his hip.

The hound's jaws parted. *You see? I said you will die.*

He growled right back. Yes, he'd die. But not before he knew Tina was safe.

"Get to the car!" he muttered to Tina, and damn it, he meant it this time.

He raised the wood, ready at bat, and smiled a crazy smile at the nails sticking out of the end. Yeah, that would hurt the mutt when it connected.

The hellhound showed its teeth and jumped. The weight of the beast sent Rick flying.

Everything melted together: the sights, the smells, the sounds. The patchy black fur of the beast, the glow of its eyes. The molten lava breath. The roar of the beast from two inches away. Tina's shrill scream. . .

For an awful, piercing minute, he thought the beast had gotten to her, because her voice went from a scream to a grumble, then built back to a roar. It went from high-pitched and feminine to gritty and mean. But Tina had to be safe, because the hellhound was on top of him, not her, and he'd wrestle the thing straight into tomorrow if it meant she could get away.

Still, something was happening where Tina stood. But he didn't dare glance her way, because the beast had his injured arm again. Rick worked his good arm up and clamped his fingers around the beast's throat, watching with satisfaction as the animal's eyes widened, registering the pain. He might die at the jaws of this beast, but a least he'd have the satisfaction of not backing down.

The hound's claws raked his chest, drawing blood. A lot of blood—he could feel it seep into his shirt, all sticky and warm. The eyes glowed brighter, like the beast knew he was going to win, and the jaws closed in on his neck.

Inevitable, the beast's eyes said. *I said I would win.*

Well, the fucker hadn't won yet. Rick shoved with everything he had left, and the beast tumbled over his shoulder, leaving him to blink at the sky. The endless blue sky of Arizona, pale and shimmery and oh so beautiful, now that he was looking at it for the last time. He flopped his head right, hoping to see Tina jumping into the car, ready to make her escape. Surely, he'd bought her enough time. Surely, she'd get away. Or maybe her family would swoop in like the cavalry right about now, armed to the teeth with a dozen shotguns to blast the hellhound into a thousand tiny bits.

He looked at Tina, then let his eyes slide shut to refocus, because something was wrong. He was all mixed up, because he was seeing a coyote where Tina should have been. No, bigger than a coyote—a wolf. A trim, black-brown wolf.

Goddamn eyesight, playing tricks on him again.

He blinked, willing his eyes to work, but the wolf was still there. Where was Tina? He searched behind the wolf. No Tina. Rolled his head farther. Still no Tina. Maybe she was crouched in the car, out of sight. A good thing, too, because he was lying in the dirt, slowly dying in the no man's land between two very angry beasts. The hellhound and its friend.

Except the newcomer wasn't the hellhound's buddy. Rick figured that out the second it started growling—not at him, but over his chest, toward the beast. Flashing white fangs and pink gums, growling like it meant business. She clawed the ground like she couldn't wait to charge and—

Wait a second. She?

Imminent death must screw with a man's mind, because not only did he have the newcomer pegged as a she-wolf, she looked strangely familiar, too. Something about the eyes. Deep, dark eyes. Beautiful eyes. Like the rest of her, all silky and shiny and purely feminine despite the fur, the fangs, the angry face.

The she-wolf stuck her nose toward him and whimpered. Then her eyes darkened and lifted to the hellhound, snuffling somewhere over his shoulder. Somewhere not too far, but he wasn't looking, because he couldn't drag his eyes off her.

She coiled, growled to high heaven, and jumped. Jumped clear over his body. Rick rolled, following the acrobatics. He winced as the wolf crashed into the hellhound. The air exploded with canine snarls and a blur of motion as they launched into combat. He watched, fascinated and strangely removed, as the two creatures battled.

The similarity between the two canines ended at four feet and a tail. The hellhound looked like a huge dog that had been resurrected and dragged out of a muddy grave, while the wolf was sleek and glossy and somehow pure, as if God had spent a good long time perfecting that project before releasing it into the world to fulfill its purpose.

A purpose which seemed to include saving Rick's ass, of all things, because the she-wolf wasn't just fighting the hellhound. She was driving it away. Every razor-toothed attack and parry of lethal claws pushed the hellhound half a step farther from him.

Why? Why would the wolf risk her life for him? He was dying anyway. Couldn't she tell?

He rolled to his stomach and worked his knees under his body, ignoring the seeping sensation in his gut. Got to his feet and swayed for a second, then focused on the fight. Tightened his fingers around the wood he'd picked up and vowed to hang in long enough to help the wolf finish the beast off.

He advanced, looking for an opening. Easier said than done, because the fighting canines were a whirlwind—a lethal, snarling whirlwind, and the hellhound was winning the upper hand. The wolf snapped and slashed and danced away, barely an inch ahead of those greedy jaws, but the hellhound was bigger—much bigger—and fueled by some unearthly energy.

It slashed at the sleek wolf's shoulder, and she howled in pain, leaping away.

Rick bounded forward and swung his makeshift weapon, catching the hellhound above the eye. He sent it sprawling, giving the she-wolf a chance to get up. She struggled to her feet and faced him with an incredulous look.

Why were those eyes so familiar? What was it about the wolf?

He didn't have time to consider, because the hellhound bellowed and launched into another attack. Rick went down swinging, because his body couldn't do it any more. He crashed to the ground as the fight continued beside, around, even over him, until he saw the she-wolf being tossed to one side. Everything slowed down and played out in a horribly slow-motion way. The hellhound turned back to his prone body. The glowing eyes honed in on his, and it nodded.

This time, you really do die.

This time, Rick believed it. There was no way out.

Chapter Twenty-Four

What was he thinking?

Tina scrambled to her feet, ignoring the pain of her wounds. She could have screamed at Rick. This was no time for courage. No time for selflessness. A human had about as much business fighting a hellhound as a lone she-wolf did. It was suicide, and yet there Rick was, charging into battle when he could have shied away.

For her. He did it for her. He'd pushed her toward the car, squared his shoulders, and faced death just to give her a chance.

Even after she'd shifted, he fought on. She'd seen the confusion in his eyes. Seen him search for the woman he knew instead of the wolf she had become. But instead of scrambling to safety when she'd given him the chance, he jumped right back into the fray.

What the hell was he doing?

He's doing what we're doing, her wolf retorted. *Fighting for our lives.*

Our lives. Plural. The team aspect was the only thing she liked about this situation, because it was utterly hopeless. She could delay the inevitable, but she could never win. Zack had said as much that day in the council house.

To kill a hellhound, you get every wolf in the county together and attack it from all sides. Hope it doesn't kill too many of you while you try to kill it.

Try? Ty had asked.

Try, Zack had echoed, looking grim.

147

Well, she was trying, but it wasn't enough. The hellhound was too big, too powerful. Even a wolf like Ty wouldn't hold out against this powerful demon for long.

The second before her shift, she'd closed her eyes and concentrated everything on sending an urgent cry to her packmates. But even the fleetest werewolf couldn't cover the fifteen miles from Twin Moon Ranch to Dead Horse Bluff at the speed she needed them to. They'd get there, all right, but they would be too late. Too late for Rick, too late for her. All she could hope for was victory for her packmates with the least possible loss of life.

She coiled every muscle and jumped at the hellhound, knocking it away from Rick. Each blow she landed was a blow that would weaken the beast, helping the others to finish it off. That's what she had to concentrate on.

She slammed into it then scrambled away from its deadly claws. Twisted her front paw in the process and earned another angry snarl from the beast. At least she'd gotten him away from Rick, who was fading fast. He'd lost too much blood, been wounded too critically. Her soul howled, knowing he was on his last legs.

The hellhound focused those deadly eyes on her, and the red flared. It advanced slowly, snarling into the ground. Yes, it was the end, all right.

Even Tex, who'd been whimpering in her car the whole time, howled. At least he would survive this horror, locked safely away. If it weren't for the dog, she'd have never found Rick, because Tex had met her at the gate of Seymour Ranch with a wagging tail and worried eyes and insisted on leading her in the direction of the back road.

Lady! Run away! poor Tex screamed. He was about as articulate a dog as existed, which wasn't saying much. But maybe he'd be articulate enough to tell the others how bravely Rick fought. How she'd tried to the bitter end.

An end that faced her now, because there was no mistaking the intent in the hellhound's eyes.

Die, she-wolf. Die.

She took a step back, wavering for the first time. Rick struggled to get up, but he was too weak now, and she cried inside. Cried for not being able to hold him, to comfort him, one more time.

That was on the inside. On the outside, she unleashed the most brutal snarl she'd ever uttered. A snarl worthy of a warrior who'd never be cowed.

Try me, you monster, she challenged the hellhound. *Try me.*

The red eyes blazed, and the creature leaped so high, smashing into her so hard, she knew that was the end. She crashed to the ground with its jaws at her neck, its body weight pinning her down on her side. Foul breath engulfed her.

You die, she-wolf, a gravelly inner voice goaded.

She'd pissed the beast off enough to make him drag it out, apparently, because the hellhound lingered there, huffing into her fur. Crushing her ribs. Drooling. Taunting her.

Cry, little she-wolf. Cry while you can.

Her teeth were too far to bite, but she bared them all the same.

Now die, little she-wolf. Die.

The hellhound dipped its head and stretched its jaws wide, honing in on her throat. Tina closed her eyes, trying to transport her thoughts elsewhere. Like Spring Hollow, all those years ago, and her very first kiss. Like the grandfather clock in the Seymour house, and waiting with the other kids for it to bong. Sitting in the sunshine on the veranda, where Rick had fed her a feast. Any of the thousand little memories she had of times with him would do. Anything but this.

The hellhound murmured in greed. It was so close to her ear, the sound echoed in her head. Grew and grew until the ground rumbled and her body shook and—

Something like a freight train thundered past her, and the hellhound's weight was lifted away. She watched it arc through the air in unnatural flight. Blinked, trying to understand. Blinked again when cloven hooves appeared. Lots of them, thundering past. Her ears filled with the sound of deep, deadly squeals and grunts. So low, she could feel the bass in her bones. Curled ivory flashed and—

Yes! her human voice cheered. Her wolf whimpered in sheer relief.

Javelinas. Wild boars.

Correction, her wolf murmured. *Javelina shifters.* Allies of Twin Moon pack.

They were big, bristly, and angrier than a trio of charging bulls. About the size of charging bulls, too; each must have topped three hundred pounds. One charged past so close she could feel the rough hide, the whoosh of air, the rush of heat.

The javelinas were all fury, all revenge, as if the hellhound had attacked a daughter of their own kind.

You should have seen these javelinas! She remembered Lana saying the first time they'd appeared in the ranch, years before. *Like no javelina I've ever seen. They were huge! Massive! All muscle. All power.*

Even coming from Lana, the superlatives had been hard to believe. But she hadn't been exaggerating. Not one bit.

The first javelina wheeled and charged the hellhound just as it found its feet. The hellhound roared and slashed with its razor claws. The boar grunted wildly and body checked it, jerking his head toward the hound's side.

Goring it. He was trying to gore the hellhound with his tusks. Tina cheered inside.

The hilltop exploded into noise as the other two javelinas closed in, screaming their fury. They worked together, driving the hellhound toward the cliff.

Yes! her wolf cried. *Push it off the cliff!* Not even a demon would survive that fall.

For all their raw power, however, the supersized javelinas struggled to win ground. The hellhound was far more agile and better armed. It could inflict damage across a wider radius with its claws and teeth, while the javelinas had to get suicidally near to gore their enemy with curved tusks that were lethal, but close to their heads. Only the foremost javelina seemed bold enough to try it. The other two worked as a dual battering ram, charging side by side. They had the look of seasoned warriors who knew how to bide their time, while the third gave every impression of a young buck, eager to prove his mettle in battle. He was quicker, bolder, more willing to take risks.

Too many risks? Tina winced as the hellhound's claws raked four parallel lines into the javelina's side. He grunted in pain and stumbled away while his brethren bulldozed in just in time.

Every thundering charge the javelinas made was met by a hellish roar, every inch won in the battle counteracted by a furious inch regained.

Jumping into the fray would be suicide, so Tina limped over to Rick and crouched over his prone form, shielding him from the kicks, the jumps, the crushing falls. She dipped her head and found his eyes. Deep, dark eyes blinking up at her, trying to comprehend.

It's me, she wanted to cry. *Me.*

Her human side screamed to shift so that she could hold his hand, cover his wounds, murmur in his ear. *I love you, Rick. Please, please hold on.*

Hold on for what, she didn't let herself think, because he was bleeding from wounds no doctor could heal.

Her wolf side growled and kept one eye on the battle, one eye on Rick, protecting her mate. *Mine!* she roared so fiercely, the hellhound and javelinas glanced her way. *My mate!*

Her incredibly brave mate, who was staring a wolf in the face without so much as a flinch. He lifted a shaky hand toward her—slowly, cautiously—and she leaned in, desperate for contact. Tentative fingers touched the outer edge of her coat, then flexed and dug closer to the skin beneath. The raging battle faded to the background, pushing everything away. It was just her and her mate. Warmth coursed between them as she willed him to understand.

It's me. I love you. I always have.

Rick's eyes went wide. His fingers dug deeper, threading through the thick ruff at her neck then sliding higher toward her jaw. Tina imagined him cupping her human face, stroking her lips.

I love you. Her voice shook, even in her mind. *I always wanted you. It killed me to say no when you asked if I would leave Arizona with you.* She pushed the thoughts his way, hoping they'd somehow register in his mind. *It wasn't you that made me say no, Rick. It was me. Me, the wolf. I couldn't go.*

His cheek twitched, and he drew in a breath so raspy, it hurt to hear.

She'd never wanted to believe in a heaven as much as she did in that moment. God, did she want to believe. That there was a peaceful, sunny place somewhere where lovers could reunite and live all the dreams they'd never gotten to enjoy in real life. A place where they'd come together in a crushing hug and never, ever be dragged apart.

But what if that place didn't exist?

She blinked back tears and licked his arm, the best she could offer in wolf form. She eased her belly to the ground, curling around him. Shielding him from the horror of the battle, letting him find heaven in the never-ending blue sky. Even a reflection of heaven would do.

Somewhere behind her, a javelina screamed in agony. Surely, death was on the way there, too. She bent her head, trying to shut it all away. The frantic grunts, the hellish snarls. Even the baying sound that announced the arrival of her pack-mates, sweeping onto the scene. Coyotes, too, from the sound of the determined yips, but she shut all that away to focus on her dying mate. Nothing mattered but him.

I love you. I love you. I love you. She whimpered it over and over. Listened to the ever-weakening thumps of his heart. Hoped for a miracle she knew would never come.

Rick's lips twitched, but no sound came. His eyes drooped, his fingers tightened on her fur.

Behind her, the battle reached fever pitch. An eerie scream pierced the air, then faded, and even Tina had to look up at it. A dozen wolves looked on as the hellhound flew over the cliff, flailing wildly at thin air. It tumbled out of sight, and a dozen wolf muzzles dipped, watching it fall. Two javelinas hurried to a fallen third, squealing in dismay.

So much pain, so much loss. Tina looked at Rick and ran a finger over his eyebrow—yes, a finger, because her wolf had let go and allowed her human side to take over at last.

The enemy was vanquished, but there were no cheers, no shouts of triumph. Only heart-crushing grief that hung over the bluff like a fog.

Chapter Twenty-Five

Tina bent over Rick, whispering. Trying to hold herself together for his sake. If nothing else, she could give him peace.

At the first touch of her fingers, his eyes widened a bit and her name fluttered from his lips.

"Tina."

She shushed him with one gentle finger, and he smiled. *Smiled*, like he wasn't bleeding from a dozen wounds or lying in the dirt at death's door. Smiled, like he couldn't think of a place he'd rather be.

Tina. She swore he repeated her name, if not aloud then in his mind. *I love you.*

I love you, too.

The smile grew. His whole face lit up, and his lips quirked, about to say something. But then his eyes grew distant. His fingers relaxed, one by one.

Her heart thumped harder, and she dropped to his chest, listening for the beat of life. It was still there, but weak. Weaker...

"Tina," somebody whispered. Someone familiar. Carly? Tina pushed the hands away. No one was going to force her away from her mate. No one!

"God, Tina," another voice whispered. Lana dropped to her knees alongside.

Tina held back a growl, protecting her mate.

A wolf snuffled closer and shook its head sadly. *Tina...*

Why couldn't everyone just go away? Couldn't they let Rick die in peace?

He won't have peace, not like this. That was Zack, reading her thoughts. His whisper penetrated her mind. *Hellhound wounds don't always kill, Tina.*

Her back went stiff. Everyone went stiff, judging by the shocked silence.

The bite of a demon can turn its prey, Zack murmured, still in wolf form.

Lana pulled back, shaking slightly. "You mean. . ."

Tina wanted to slap her hands over her ears and scream.

Sometimes, the victim doesn't die, Zack said. *The strong ones hang on. . .*

Rick was strong. She could feel his heart, soldiering on.

Some hang on with a little bit of demon poison in them, and they slowly turn. Like this hellhound. It must have been a shifter before.

"You mean. . ." Lana trailed off, aghast.

Everyone stared at Tina, perhaps wondering if she was going to turn into a beast, too.

Zack shook his head. *It's rare, but it happens to those who reach the edge of death. If the power of the poison kicks in, they tip back to life. As a demon. Demons in human shape. Demons in the form of animals. . .*

"No wonder the hellhound looked so. . . sick. So scrappy." Lana shook her head.

Horrible images assaulted Tina's mind. Images of Rick— kind, pure-hearted Rick—slowly losing his mind. Slowly going mad. Going evil. Hurting others. . .

No, no! It couldn't be.

We have to finish him off, Zack said. *Make sure he dies before the poison makes him tip back.*

She threw herself over Rick's chest. No way was anyone touching her mate!

"Tina." A hand closed over her shoulder. Cody murmured in his softest but most insistent voice. "Tina, you have to let go."

No, no, no! She shoved her brother away.

"We have to, Tina. He'll become like it."

Bile rose in her throat. *Not Rick. Please, not him. . .*

"We have to, Tina," Cody went on. "He wouldn't want it."

Tina nearly jumped up then, ready to kick and hit and scream. But just as she gathered herself, a pair of wolves hurried in.

No! Heather barked, pushing Cody aside. *How can you even suggest such a thing?*

No! Stef growled, flanking Heather. *How could you do that to your mate?*

There was a stunned kind of silence until Cody blurted one word. "Mate?"

Yes! Tina wanted to scream. *Yes, even your spinster sister has the right to a mate, damn it! A destined mate.*

But she didn't have to say anything, because Carly—Carly, of all people!—did it for her. "Her destined mate," her sister said in a reverent tone that carried over the hills.

"Oh, God," Lana whispered. "Your destined mate?"

Tina read the unspoken words going through everyone's minds. A dozen heads shook sadly. *Poor, poor Tina. All these years, hiding her love for Rick, and now...*

She gritted her teeth, ready to shift back into wolf form and fight them all away. To fight for some shred of hope or comfort amidst the horror of it all.

"Look, it's not like I want to kill him," Cody tried. "But—"

Wait!

Another she-wolf darted closer, ears held high in defiance. She moved in quick, flighty steps. It was Rae, urgent and edgy in a way Tina had never seen her before.

Tina, Rae urged, *bite him!*

"No!" This time, she really did scream it out loud.

"Are you nuts?" Lana stared at Rae.

Not bite to kill! Rae barked. *I mean a mating bite!*

A ripple of surprise went through the gathered pack, and Tina felt a spark jump inside her chest. *The mating bite...*

A mating bite! Rae said it again. *If it works fast enough, he'll heal. It'll bring him back from the edge and keep him safe.*

Zack shook his head in a fierce no. *It's a one-in-a-million chance the change will come fast enough to work.*

Tina's eyes jumped to Rick's face. If he weren't so pale, she might have imagined he was only asleep. Peaceful, unworried. Unaware.

One in a million. Zack shook his head.

Tina studied Rick, the love of her life. If he wasn't one in a million, who was?

Our mate is strong! her wolf screamed inside. *It could work!*

"If it doesn't work..." Cody said, still skeptical.

Heather butted him aside with an angry huff. *Would you do it for me?*

"Hell, yeah," Cody retorted. "But—"

There is no but, Heather cut in. *She has to try.*

Try. The word made Tina cower.

You have to believe, Rae said.

She wanted to throw back her head and howl. The bite of a wolf could kill a man—especially a strong man, whose body would resist the change.

"He's dying anyway," Carly whispered.

Tina shook. If she bit him and he died, she'd feel responsible forever. If she bit him and the demon venom still took over, the scenario was even worse. She'd be mated to a man who'd slowly go mad and become a demon himself.

"It's too risky." Ty cut in. "Better for everyone that we finish him off now."

Lana yelped, but Ty went on.

"Look," he said, and his voice cracked. "Tina, I wish..."

Her rock of a brother, pleading with her in that apologetic tone. In any other situation, she'd have been moved to tears.

"She has to try," Lana insisted.

Cody and Ty exchanged hard looks then curt nods. Tina read the message in their eyes. *If it doesn't work, we'll rip him to pieces the moment we're sure.*

Did she really want to witness that?

You have to believe, Rae whispered, pulling Tina's focus back to Rick.

Mate! Mine! her wolf cried.

She leaned over Rick's neck, mourning already, because it shouldn't be like this. She'd imagined exchanging mating bites with Rick in a thousand dusky dreams, but it was nothing like this. Mating should be an intimate, joyous event, not a moment of despair. It should be two souls agreeing to join as one, not one wolf forcing her way upon another.

You have to believe, Rae whispered, more urgently.

Tina's wolf reared up inside her. Her canines pushed against her gums, extending for the bite. She leaned closer and closed her eyes, inhaling Rick's rich musk. Her tongue swiped his neck, honing in on the faint pulse. Finding the spot.

Mate! Mine! her wolf howled. *Take him!*

Forgive me, my love, she whispered, if only in her mind. *Forgive me.*

More gently than any love-struck wolf would think possible, Tina let her teeth sink in.

You have to believe. Rae's words echoed in her mind.

She closed her eyes and held him, trying to believe.

Trying. Trying. Trying...

Chapter Twenty-Six

Rick drifted through shadow and flickering light. His chest ached, his arm throbbed. His shoulder cried. His neck was warm and tingly, though, and that made up for the rest. The pain faded in and out, and in the blissful peace in between, an out-of-nowhere slide show clicked through his mind.

He saw the Seymours, rocking on their porch swing. Smiling, shooting the breeze, inhaling the setting sun like the breath of life.

Click. A Thanksgiving dinner from long ago, or maybe lots of Thanksgiving dinners blurred into one massive feast. The mouth-watering smell of roast turkey wafting from the kitchen. Cranberries, sweet potatoes, and the sugary scent of an apple pie, cooling on a windowsill. His dad, smiling while he handed Rick dishes to set the Seymours' mile-long table. The steady bong of the grandfather clock, making his pulse spike, because the guests would be there soon. Tina would be there soon.

Click. A new image. Riding out into the desert on Blue the brown horse, feeling like the world belonged to him, because Tina was there on Star, and she was smiling at him.

One perfect memory after another flitted through his mind, pushing the pain far, far away, along with that dark fog that hung around the edges of his thoughts. The one that threatened to creep in and steal some part of his soul if he didn't keep that slide show running, with all its golden images. He couldn't let the slide show stop.

Click. Sunrise on the veranda of the Seymours' house. Him and Tina, sipping coffee, watching the pink fade from the sky. He knew damn well it wasn't a memory, that one. Just a fantasy, and somehow, he wasn't ready for that yet. So he clicked on to another image. Sunrise, in the apartment over the barn. Something warm and safe snuggled by his leg. His mind made it Tina, cuddled close.

Yeah, that was a good one. He'd stay on that slide for as long as he could.

Which he did a damn good job of, apparently, because even after he'd drifted through what felt like days and finally awoke, it was in exactly that way—with something warm and safe snuggled by his leg.

He cracked an eye open, ready to caress Tina's glossy black-brown hair.

Damn it, though, his eyes were playing tricks again, because they registered a dog there. Not Tex. Bigger. Darker. A rich, earthy mixture of black and brown, like the most fertile soil in the fields of farmers' dreams.

A really, really big dog, with really beautiful eyes.

He blinked. Closed his eyes. Drifted for another couple of days. Every time he woke up for a few seconds before exhaustion pulled him back to the slide show, the dog was there. He started petting it, because the poor thing sure looked like it could use some petting, being all sad and tragic as it was. One by one, he walked his fingers across the crisp white sheets of whatever comfy bed he was in, and then buried them in that warm fur, stroking quietly. If he managed to keep it up long enough, he even imagined a purr. A nice, cozy purr that put him right back to sleep.

The fog bank seemed to break up, at least in the weird weather dome that had taken over his mind, with a little sunshine peeking through in patches that came and went. He started hearing voices, too.

"Wounds closing nicely..." said a kind and gentle voice with a tiny shake in it, like a sweet old grandmother or older aunt.

"No sign of...?" asked a second voice, trailing off into uncertainty. Another old lady who seemed terribly worried about something so bad, she didn't dare say what it was.

A dry, wrinkled hand patted his arm soothingly, like he was the one who'd been worried.

"No sign, thank goodness," said the first woman. "It'll be all right."

He wondered what there was that might have gone wrong, and the fog bank came to mind. The one that was only a distant memory, because the sun was shining in the weather dome.

"How's our other patient?" the worried one asked.

Patient? Crap, was he back in the trauma ward? What if the last couple of months were all just a dream?

"He'll survive. They're tough, his kind. But my goodness, it was close. It'll be a long, slow recovery."

Rick wondered who the poor guy was and what kind of accident he'd been in.

Not an accident, gut instinct told him. *A fight.*

He'd have liked to puzzle that one out, but weariness washed over him again, and he slept some more. Lots more, dreaming of bad wolves and good ones and huge, vicious boars. Until his body finally decided that enough was enough, and he woke up. Just woke up, like any other day, stretching his legs and swinging them off the bed while blinking and thinking about coffee and maybe a really, really big steak, and—

"Rick."

His head snapped up and he squinted around the room.

Not his room. Not his apartment over the barn. Not Seymour Ranch.

When he sniffed, a thousand mixed scents engulfed him as if sweet old Lucy Seymour had just thrown a window open to her garden on the finest day of spring. He would have sat there inhaling it like a good, strong cup of coffee for another hour or two if it wasn't for that voice.

Tina. She sat at the edge of his bed, and though it tore his heart out to see the dark rings around her eyes, it also made his whole body sing. Like she was the spring and he was the songbird.

Of course, songbirds didn't lunge into huge, desperate hugs the way he pulled Tina in, crushing her against his chest. Holding her, sniffing her, possessing her. Maybe even growling a tiny bit, because even if he was a little cloudy on what had happened to get him into that bed, he had the gut-sinking feeling it was something pretty bad. Something that could have ripped her away from him forever.

"Rick," she murmured.

The teary whisper was an echo of a much more frantic cry. He held her closer as images assaulted his mind. The mine. Dale. A shotgun. The beast with red eyes. Tina, screaming...

It all came back in a flood so powerful, he had to voice it, because damn, that had been close. "Dale... The wolf..."

She stiffened in his arms, but he babbled on.

"You were there but then you were gone. And I was looking for you, but there was only a wolf. Not the bad one, but another one and—"

"Rick."

Her eyes caught his, and he froze. Even his heart stopped for that split second of realization. No way. No way could she be—

"Let me explain..." Her voice was quiet and shaky, but her eyes were resolute. Sad, but resolute. "Let me explain."

His brain slipped into slow-motion mode, the way it sometimes used to do when he was at bat, focusing on one thing. Except that instead of concentrating on a ball flying his way, he was concentrating on the truth hurtling mercilessly at him. He pictured the scene at Dead Horse Bluff. Remembered turning around to see Tina gone and a wolf standing in her place.

"I have to show you something..."

He really, really wanted that to be something a lot less crazy than what his mind was suggesting right now.

She slid off the bed and started unbuttoning her blouse, though he hardly noticed, because his eyes were on her hair. Brown-black, like the desert at night. Just like the good wolf of his dreams.

He sniffed the air, and something inside him nodded. Smelled the same, too. A perfect match.

A little unsettling, because when had he ever relied on scent to match identities before?

"Please, trust me that this is okay," Tina went on, sounding so terrified of what she was doing that he nearly pulled her into another hug. But he couldn't, because she was pushing her jeans down now, absolutely, positively dedicated to the truth.

A truth he wasn't sure he was quite ready for.

The ghost of old Henry Seymour leaned in and whispered in one ear. *Good folk, all right,* he'd once said, watching the Hawthornes head home late on Thanksgiving night. *But there's something different about them.*

"Please, Rick. Trust me," Tina whispered.

He stared into her eyes. Then his jaw swung open, because she ducked her head, curved her naked back, and sank to the floor.

"Tina?"

He didn't quite get her whole name out. Not with Tina blurring gracefully into something else, a little like pulling off a winter coat. Or rather, pulling a winter coat on. A second skin.

Wolf skin.

Tina shook, and the coat shook, too, so realistically he could have sworn the good wolf was back and staring up at him with imploring eyes. Eyes just like Tina's.

He looked at her, perfectly still. Okay, maybe blinking a little. His mouth opened and closed, and he swallowed hard. His eyes weren't tricking him. Not this time.

A wolf. He thought he'd be prepared for anything, but...

His heart thumped so loudly, he could swear the roof shook.

The wolf blinked, then drooped in dejection, and what should have been a magnificent creature turned into a quivering mess.

His heart twisted at the sight. "Come here," a voice whispered. *His* voice, which was funny, because his brain seemed to be mired in mud three feet deep. But it must have been him, because his hand beckoned at the same time.

Step by slow step, the wolf advanced. Crouched. Its eyes were averted, the tail low. Rick's gut twisted, knowing it was him doing that to her.

Her. Tina.

Dios mio.

He could hear his father's voice in his mind. But it was an awed kind of call to God, not a frightened call for protection. The glossy fur was Tina's hair, just spread over more of her body. The gliding step, even in her agitation, echoed her human grace, and the face held all the intelligence of the woman he loved.

How could he be anything but awed by what she'd just done, at what she became? Sports arenas around the world filled with cheering fans who thought that hitting, throwing, or kicking a ball was an amazing trick. He'd been paid seven figures for a couple of seconds at bat a few times a week. But that was nothing—nothing!—compared to *this*.

Tina advanced another shaky step, tall yet wary.

He extended one shaky hand. Slowly, carefully. Wondering what damage those jaws might inflict. But if it was Tina...

Jesus. Tina, a wolf?

When his nose twitched with the urge to sniff, he rubbed it hard enough to make the feeling go away. Instead, he willed his hand forward. Slowly cupped the delicate muzzle as his heart thumped harder then gradually slowed. He stroked the silky nose. Looked into her eyes, and Christ, there was his princess. Maybe not locked in a tower like he'd imagined, but in a different kind of cage.

A cage he wouldn't have guessed at in a thousand years.

There's something different about them.

If only Henry knew how true those words were.

Tina blinked sadly, and in her eyes he saw the same hope and fear that tingled in his veins. And suddenly, it all made sense. Her rejections over the years. That *something* that had always held her back from embracing what she desired and deserved.

She looked so... so *rejected*, his heart wept.

"Hey, beautiful," he whispered, because she was. Tina could turn into a porcupine and she'd still be his perfect princess.

The wolf closed her eyes and leaned into his hand, just the way human Tina had leaned into his hand the few times she'd let herself give in to the pull that drew them together, again and again. He closed his eyes, too, because he didn't need to feel the hope thrumming through the room. Closed his eyes and let her edge closer and share her warmth with him. She nuzzled his hand, his arm, his shoulder...

He opened his eyes, and it was human Tina again, nuzzling him, jaw to jaw, her eyes closed as if under a magic spell. Then she sighed a little and pulled back shyly.

"Hey," he whispered.

He drew her back into a hug, because that worried look she wore just wouldn't do.

"Hey," he murmured again, taking over the nuzzling now that she'd stopped.

"This is why..." She trailed off.

He nodded into her flowing hair. "Why you always said no."

She nodded and gulped. "Rick, you almost died."

He pulled her closer and tried to joke it off. "Didn't, though."

She pulled away and kneaded her lips together, trying to find the right words. "Wolves are different."

He laughed out loud. "No kidding." Then he smiled at her and traced her eyebrows. "But maybe not so different."

She shook her head so vehemently, it worried him. What was it she didn't want to say? Did she and her siblings turn into wolves and become bloodthirsty killers? Somehow he doubted that. The Hawthornes had always had their own honor code; any good cowboy could see that.

"Just you and your family?" he ventured.

She shook her head. "All of us. All of the ranch."

Somehow, it didn't shock him. It made sense. The residents of Twin Moon Ranch had always been secretive, and there'd been a lot of wolf howls mixed in with the warble of coyotes under a full moon. Which was unusual for Arizona, but that was just the way it was, and it had been accepted by locals as a quirk of nature for years.

He wasn't sure whether to laugh or shake. Quirk of nature. Right.

Tina's eyes were filled with terror, though—terror that he'd reject who she was. He tugged her hand up and brushed his lips over her knuckles. God, she smelled good. Like the scent wafting in from outside, rich with a thousand nuanced flavors he'd barely been aware of before.

Wait. Before what?

He wasn't sure he wanted to know.

"Rick," Tina murmured, truly mournful now. "That's not all."

He held his breath. She had more for him to digest than the fact that she could transform into a wolf?

"You would have died, so I had to... I had to..."

He tilted his head at her. What could be so bad? She was alive, he was alive...

She stumbled and fumbled until finally releasing a torrent of words. "The hellhound could have turned you—"

Turned him? He didn't have time to ask, because Tina rushed ahead.

"—if I didn't do anything so I had to do it—"

Do what?

"—but it meant a mating bite—"

Whoa. A mating *what*?

"—so now you'll be a shifter like us and be mated to me and..." She broke down for a second, then hurried on. "You could have had anyone. Now you're stuck with me."

He didn't understand half of what she'd said, but he sure got the last part.

"I don't want anyone. I only want you. I've never wanted anyone but you."

She shook her head. "Really stuck, Rick. Like forever."

"I want to be stuck with you. I want forever."

"But there's so much you don't understand," she mumbled.

Her face glistened with tears that hurt to see, so he wiped them away. Pulled her tight against his chest and listened to her thumping heart.

His heart thumped too, and a deep voice murmured inside. *Mate. My mate.*

He shrugged it away, because he was tired again. Really tired. Couldn't he deal with the details some other time? "What is there to understand other than I get to be with you?"

Tina shook her head. Her gaze was fierce again. "It means you'll be a..."

He waited. A what? He wasn't thinking too clearly any more.

"...I mean, I had to bite you, so it means..."

He ran a hand down her arm to steady her a little, even though her look said she'd better steady him for whatever it was that was coming next.

"It means you'll be a wolf, too."

It took two more long, smooth strokes over her arm before the words registered. He looked at her, waiting for the punch line.

She held his gaze. No punch line, apparently.

It means you'll be a wolf, too...

He looked at her. Looked at his hands. Looked at the floor then out the window to a patch of startlingly blue sky. A wolf, huh?

He took a long, slow breath. Now, shoot. He'd need a hell of a lot more than twenty days to digest that one.

Epilogue

Two months later...

"Howdy, neighbor!" Cody grinned and extended his hand. Tina slid out of the pickup at the same time as Rick and watched the two men shake hands. It still gave her a thrill to see Rick be welcomed to Twin Moon Ranch as an equal. Hell, seeing Rick welcomed to Twin Moon in any capacity would have been a thrill. But this...this still made her glow.

She glowed even more when Ty ambled up with a curt, "Hey." Her taciturn brother hadn't waited for Rick to come to him but was paying the ultimate sign of respect, one alpha to another, by coming over to greet Rick at the car. Okay, his greeting was a single syllable, but Ty was Ty.

"Hello." Rick nodded and threw Tina a secret smile. Yeah, he had Ty figured out, too. "Happy Thanksgiving."

"Uncle Rick! Uncle Rick!" Tana and Holly ran up to him, and he swept both girls up in his arms.

"Hey! Look what I caught here! A couple of little fish!"

"We're not fish," Tana giggled and wriggled away. "We're wolves."

"Don't look like wolves to me," Rick said.

Tina's heart did a little flip, hearing how casually he said it. Like he'd been a wolf all his life.

"Yeah," Cody chuckled. "Really little, really loud wolves."

"I'm not little!" Tana insisted.

"Me, neither!" Holly added.

Tina stood for a moment, watching Rick carry his tiny charges toward the dining hall. Her beloved mate, her nieces, her brothers. Family, all together in one place.

"I still think you're fish," Rick insisted.

She laughed out loud, more at the joy in the scene than at his words.

Ty was watching, too, and he might even have let a smile slip if she hadn't glanced at him just then. He kicked at the dirt then called after Rick. "Gotta talk to you about that new project before dinner."

"Will do," Rick called. "Will do."

Tina bit back a sigh. Her list of things to be thankful for was a mile long. Rick's quick adaptation to becoming a shifter stood at the very top, followed by dozens of other points, like the fact that he and Ty were actually getting along. And not only that, but moving past the grudging détente of their early days to something approaching a respectful business partnership.

"Remember Thanksgivings with the Seymours?" she murmured, watching Rick head into the dining hall.

"Sure do." Ty nodded, then shook his head. "Damn thing, that will of old Lucy's. Full of surprises."

"You can say that again."

She'd been shocked the day the estate lawyer called not long after the hellhound attack. Rick had mended enough to move back to Seymour Ranch, and she'd moved with him, counting her luck every second. They'd been wrapped cozily around each other in the apartment above the barn when the phone rang.

"What?" Rick had shouted into the mouthpiece. He half sat, half fell onto the bed. "Are you sure?"

Old Lucy Seymour hadn't just named him manager of the ranch. She'd also named him sole heir in a clause that said if Rick did a solid job his first twenty days on the job, the ranch would be his.

"Bless the Seymours and their twenty-day rule," Tina murmured, nodding at her brother.

"Twenty days?" Ty asked.

She waved a vague hand. Someday, she'd try to explain.

Rick had joked about his first twenty days as a wolf, but the amazing thing was, he'd taken to it by the end of his second shift.

Check this out. Rick had grinned at her in his new wolf form and took off flying down a scrubby slope, teeth bared in glee. They'd run for hours before stopping to howl their joy to the moon in a duet that went on and on, and then wrapped up a memorable night by making love under the stars. As wolves, then as humans, when Rick worked up the nerve to bite deep into her flesh and seal their mating bond forever.

"You sure I won't hurt you?" he'd asked.

"I'm sure." God, was she sure.

When his teeth sank into her neck, sparks hammered through her, and her whole body shook with pleasure. With relief, too. Her destined mate was hers—truly hers—at last.

"No wonder Dale wanted him dead," Ty grunted, pulling her back into the present.

Tina shivered at the thought. Lucy Seymour's will had also stipulated that if Rick were deemed unsuitable as manager, the entire ranch would go to Dale.

She shook her head at the ugly image of what Dale would have done with beautiful Seymour Ranch, like selling its precious resources to the highest bidder. Water, gold, uranium. Who knew what else the man had planned?

"You two serious about bringing in that new Heritage breed Henry used to talk about?" Ty asked.

She smiled. She and Rick had plans to work Seymour Ranch by honest means, mixing tradition with innovation. Hard work and honest enterprise were the way to a prosperous future, not raping the earth. They might never get rich doing it, but hey, she already had all the riches she wanted.

Well, almost all. She watched Carly scurry up with a squirming baby Sammie in her arms. From the look of it, Carly had had enough of babysitting for Heather and Cody.

"Can I hold her?" Tina blurted.

Carly laughed and handed the baby over. "Hello to you, too, favorite sister. And yes, please! I'm at the end of my patience here."

Ty snorted. "Already?"

"Hey!" Carly protested. "This is a lot of work!"

"Just you wait," Ty murmured and ambled off, dodging Carly's play-slap. "Just you wait."

"Like I'll ever have kids." Carly huffed at his back. "And hey, if you're not nice to me, I won't stay for this long a visit ever again."

"Promise?" Ty shot back.

Tina tuned out the amiable sibling banter and hugged Sammie close. Inhaled her soft baby scent. Marveled at the tiny fingers, the plump cheeks. Wondered if she was being greedy for wanting even *more* joy in her life. But there was a time and place for everything, so she'd be patient a little longer. She had a ranch to sort out, a mate to shower with love, and a challenging job as head accountant and chief operations officer of two ranches.

Plus a brand-new he-wolf to show the ropes, her wolf added in a lusty undertone. *In bed and out.*

Right. Like Rick needed any teaching when it came to *that.* Even in wolf form, the guy was a natural.

Oh, there's still a trick or two I can teach my mate. The wolf grinned, giving its tail an imaginary swipe.

My mate. She could live a hundred years and still tingle from the power of those two words.

Carly leaned in. "Promise me we'll do Thanksgiving at your place next year."

Tina lifted an eyebrow. "Why's that?"

Carly flipped her ponytail over her shoulder. "Less cleanup, of course."

"Maybe for you." Tina's voice was scolding, but she swelled inside at the image. Thanksgiving at her new home. The Seymour homestead would come alive again with voices, footsteps, and chatter. The garden she'd been laboring to revive would need another couple of seasons, but it was coming along nicely. The whole ranch was, bit by bit.

She pictured her relatives arriving, crowding the long table, passing platters laden with food. The solemn voice of the grandfather clock would fascinate another generation of Hawthorne kids, and the house would fill with laughter. Mrs. Seymour would be proud, and Tina might just feel ready to call herself lady of the house.

Not that she and Rick had actually moved in to the main house yet. They'd decided to settle in together in the apartment over the barn and move to the house after the holidays. A new year, a new beginning. She couldn't wait.

Her eyes swept over Twin Moon Ranch. The mighty cottonwoods, the chirping crickets, the gentle breeze. A horse whinnied in the distance, and a stray chicken pecked at the dirt. A dog snoozed in the shade. The smell of barbecue permeated the air, because the guys had the grill going, as if the usual Thanksgiving trimmings wouldn't be enough. She closed her eyes and breathed it all in.

Home.

Twin Moon Ranch had always felt like it stood in the crosshairs of a rifle, with danger all around. But for the first time, it felt secure, as if they'd built a moat. Their alliance with the coyote shifters of Echo Creek was stronger than ever. Now that Seymour Ranch had joined that alliance, too, everyone had gained firmer footing than ever. The three territories together covered a huge chunk of central Arizona, creating a formidable force. Maybe even a new era of peace for her pack.

"If you don't watch out, life might just get boring," Carly murmured, reading her thoughts.

"Right, boring." Tina shook her head. Two huge ranches to run, a new pack to establish, a new partnership to manage...

My mate to take care of, her wolf chimed in, setting off the tingle again.

Yeah, she'd take that kind of *boring* any day.

"And just think—now Dad will want to meddle with your ranch, too." Carly chuckled. "He's only staying in Colorado until North Ridge finds a suitable alpha to run the pack. Then he'll be right back here, making a nuisance of himself."

Tina thought it over. "No. I mean, yes, Dad will make a nuisance of himself. But he'll be happy, too." Because the unthinkable had happened: another shifter pack had established itself in the area without a drop of blood spilled—well, at least not between warring shifters. Her father had always harped on about the advantages of joint territories, though he'd never, ever have tolerated another alpha anywhere near his home turf. He could hardly object to a new pack forming at Seymour Ranch, though, not with his own daughter as alpha female there. In fact, her dad couldn't have orchestrated a more advantageous alliance if he'd tried.

Funny, the way fate worked sometimes.

"Right. Dad, happy. That I gotta see." Carly chuckled. "The man is only happy when he's unhappy."

"True," Tina murmured. Painfully true. But her dad would just have to learn to butt out. Seymour pack would be Rick's to run, just like the ranch, and she'd be at his side every step of the way. They'd need a lot of new hires to wrestle the ranch into shape, but they'd have their pick of young shifters eager to make a new start with a promising new pack.

Her pack.

She sighed and let her eyes drift a little more then snuggled her cheek against little Sammie's. Twin Moon Ranch would always be home, but Seymour Ranch was, too. Bit by bit, everything was falling into place.

"Ugh," Carly muttered.

"What?"

"You've got that dreamy look again. I'm starting to feel sick." She sauntered toward the dining hall.

"Ka!" Sammie motioned in an order to follow. *Ka* for Carly, because Carly's magnetism even drew babies in.

Tina twirled a finger in the baby's downy hair and followed Carly out of the bright daylight and into the soothing shade of the dining hall. Oak tables formed three lines across the cool flagstone floor, and most the pack was already gathered, ready to eat. Their happy chatter filled the airy space between thick beams that supported a high ceiling, decorated with colorful flags. Packmates raised their hands in welcoming waves and little cheers of hello. A few, like her Aunt Jean and old Ruth, gestured toward Rick with winks of approval.

Yes, everything was falling into place.

Axel, the injured javelina shifter, was propped up in a place of honor near the fireplace. Tina strode over to him, at a loss for words as always, because how could she ever thank the man who'd given her a beautiful future instead of a horrible end? Little Tana and Holly had abandoned Rick to tend to Axel, their newest hero. Everyone's hero, in fact, and Tina's most of all. If it hadn't been for the javelina's courage on the day of the hellhound attack...

"Happy Thanksgiving, Axel," she murmured, trying to make her thanks seep into every word.

"Happy Thanksgiving," the burly man croaked in his deep, earthy voice.

"Brought you cookies," she said.

"My favorite," Axel rumbled, hitting a seven or eight on the Richter scale with his deep voice. He smiled as he always did, no matter what kind of cookies they were. She'd baked enough for him in the past weeks to feed an army. Visited him daily as he recuperated, too, though it still would never seem like enough.

Javelinas were tough—and the amiable Axel doubly so— but they healed slowly. The young boar had a long road ahead of him to recovery. The least Twin Moon Ranch could do was host him while he convalesced. When the time came, he could head back to the nomadic life of his kind.

Not that the modest javelina shifter looked ready to rush off anytime soon. Not with those injuries, and certainly not with half the pack's single females doting on his every move. The poor guy didn't have the energy to evade them even if he wanted to.

Uh-oh. An urgent murmur sounded in Tina's mind.

She spun to see Lana tilting her head toward the head table, where Ty and Rick sat in animated conversation. Uh-oh, indeed.

Not good, Lana warned, already striding over on long legs, ready to rein Ty in.

Tina handed Sammie to Aunt Jean, steeled herself for trouble, and race-walked over. Alpha males who hadn't yet fully established their respective ranks had a way of jumping straight from conversation into all-out war. Tina and Lana reached the table at exactly the same moment, and each slid a placating hand over her mate's shoulder. Lana had a lot of practice with the gesture, and though it was new to Tina, she felt like she'd been doing it all her life.

Rick's hand found hers, and as always, his touch was a bridge that connected their souls.

"Hey, Tina, Lana. Good thing you're here," Ty said.

Yeah, Lana's wink said. *Good thing we're here.*

"Where do you reckon is the best place to put the new pump house?"

Tina blinked. From the sounds of it, the men hadn't been on the verge of a territorial dispute. More like an amicable business talk.

"The new pump house?" she mumbled.

"Why operate two leaky pump houses when we can share one? A new, efficient one," Rick chimed in, and both men looked up, waiting for her reaction.

Lana waited, too, and Tina warmed all over. Maybe Good Old Tina wasn't just a quiet supporter. Maybe she was a leader in her own right.

Rick squeezed her hand, and Lana gave her a wry smile as if she'd known it all along.

"Um... The spot just west of where the old one stood seems like a good one, and it was on Stef's list of recommended sites," she managed.

"Exactly what I was thinking." Rick nodded.

Ty nodded, too. "Just need to work out the details. Fifty-fifty split of costs and water?" He looked at Rick.

"Sounds good to me."

"Just don't get greedy and talk about increasing the volume," Lana warned.

Ty waved a hand. "No way."

Rick dipped his head in agreement. "Not going there."

"Hey, everyone, dig in!" Cody announced from across the hall. The feast was on.

The children scampered over, along with all the young men of the pack who seemed to inhale food the way they inhaled air.

The old curmudgeons leaned back and waited at their table, waxing poetic about the good old days.

Good old days? Tina sighed and looked around. More like good new days. The ranch was prospering, the kids happy and healthy. Christmas was right around the corner, and it would be a truly special one.

She couldn't help it. She leaned over and kissed Rick, full on the lips. Hung on to that kiss and lost herself in her mate's taste. She let it go a little deeper. Slid her hands down his shoulders and slowly settled into his lap.

What did it matter if Cody cleared his throat in an amused hint, or that the little girls giggled, or the old ladies sighed dreamily? Nothing was going to make her break that kiss. She deserved that kiss. She deserved Rick.

At long, long last, she had her mate.

When she finally pulled back and rested her forehead on his, she whispered. "Mine. Mate." Inside, her wolf swished its tail in long, dreamy strokes.

Rick's face glowed like he'd just swung his way into the Baseball Hall of Fame. "Mine," he echoed, even louder, letting the whole world hear. "Mate."

Sneak Peek: Desert Rose

An expected hero comes home — but can he stay?

Axel Waldermann's days in paradise are numbered, and he knows it. The last thing this reluctant hero needs is temptation in the form of a curvy she-wolf. One step too close, one kiss too many, and he'll shatter the fragile alliance between his shifter clan and the powerful wolves of Twin Moon pack. But with destiny whispering in his ears and desire pumping through his veins, how can he resist?

Every local girl has her sights set on Axel, the most eligible bachelor in town. So what chance does an unassuming girl like Beth Carter have? When a deadly enemy lures Axel into the fight of his life, Beth will have to test her limits and believe not just in love, but in herself. Can this desert rose become a heroine and win her destined mate?

Don't miss the passion, suspense, or romance. Get your copy of DESERT ROSE today!

Books by Anna Lowe

The Wolves of Twin Moon Ranch

Desert Hunt (the Prequel)

Desert Moon (Book 1)

Desert Blood (Book 2)

Desert Fate (Book 3)

Desert Heart (Book 4)

Desert Rose (Book 5)

Desert Roots (Book 6)

Desert Yule (a short story)

Desert Wolf: Complete Collection (Four short stories)

Sasquatch Surprise (a Twin Moon spin-off story)

Aloha Shifters - Jewels of the Heart

Lure of the Dragon (Book 1)

Lure of the Wolf (Book 2)

Lure of the Bear (Book 3)

Lure of the Tiger (Book 4)

Love of the Dragon (Book 5)

Lure of the Fox (Book 6)

Aloha Shifters - Pearls of Desire

Rebel Dragon (Book 1)

Rebel Bear (Book 2)

Rebel Lion (Book 3)

Rebel Wolf (Book 4)

Rebel Heart (A prequel to Book 5)

Rebel Alpha (Book 5)

Fire Maidens - Billionaires & Bodyguards

Fire Maidens: Paris (Book 1)

Fire Maidens: London (Book 2)

Fire Maidens: Rome (Book 3)

Fire Maidens: Portugal (Book 4)

Fire Maidens: Ireland (Book 5)

Blue Moon Saloon

Perfection (a short story prequel)

Damnation (Book 1)

Temptation (Book 2)

Redemption (Book 3)

Salvation (Book 4)

Deception (Book 5)

Celebration (a holiday treat)

Shifters in Vegas

Paranormal romance with a zany twist

Gambling on Trouble

Gambling on Her Dragon

Gambling on Her Bear

Serendipity Adventure Romance

Off the Charts

Uncharted

Entangled

Windswept

Adrift

Travel Romance

Veiled Fantasies

Island Fantasies

visit www.annalowebooks.com

About the Author

USA Today and Amazon bestselling author Anna Lowe loves putting the "hero" back into heroine and letting location ignite a passionate romance. She likes a heroine who is independent, intelligent, and imperfect – a woman who is doing just fine on her own. But give the heroine a good man – not to mention a chance to overcome her own inhibitions – and she'll never turn down the chance for adventure, nor shy away from danger.

Anna loves dogs, sports, and travel – and letting those inspire her fiction. On any given weekend, you might find her hiking in the mountains or hunched over her laptop, working on her latest story. Either way, the day will end with a chunk of dark chocolate and a good read.

Visit AnnaLoweBooks.com